English Slacker

GW00500554

Chris Morton

Punked Books

Published in 2011 by Punked Books
An Authortrek imprint

Punked Books
C/O Authortrek
PO Box 54168
London
W5 9EE
(FAQ via www.authortrek.com/punked-books)

First Edition

ONE

It was a beautiful day actually, probably the first of the summer. I felt like doing something before work so I phoned up Alex and Paul to see what they were up to, which I knew wouldn't be much and they dropped round just as I was finishing breakfast.

They didn't come in or anything. Paul stayed in the van and Alex was like hovering at the door saying, "Let's go," and even though I'd kinda pictured us sitting in the porch for a bit before going out (my mum had gone to work by then) I thought, "Fuck it," and went back to the kitchen shouting, "Okay, I'll be out in a minute!"

I downed my tea, picked up the remaining bits of toast I had left and quickly ran back to the front door to find them already in the van, music blaring out and that, the whole road listening. And yeah, as I approached I could soon see the thick smoke coming out of the windows.

I got in the van – Alex sliding the door closed behind me, Paul saying, "Hey Chambers," from the front – and sat down on the sofa-seat, still holding my toast. Alex said, "Hey man, are you okay?" and Paul said, "Yeah man, you all right?" and I replied, "Yeah," to both of them but that was it. No direct mention of Colin or anything. I remember this distinctly.

So anyway, we'd planned to park up the road and smoke a few in the back of the van but it was too damn hot in there, even with the windows open. So after a while we started driving around, looking for a nice place to enjoy the sunshine.

Alex told us stories of his night out before, about this Skipton bird he'd met who was, "Fuckin' nuts," once he'd got her, "in the sack."

From what he was saying it did sound pretty funny. Apparently she'd been pissed off with a friend for hooking up with some guy in her year she didn't like and had totally gone for Alex just to outdo her mate and that. Basically, at least from the way he was telling it, Alex had very much had

3

it on a plate. I remember Paul getting more and more jealous as Alex went into the details, asking him questions about what she was wearing, how big her tits were and Alex was well enjoying winding him up.

It wasn't long before Alex passed me the joint, after which I started to feel quite relaxed; not surprising considering how much he'd packed in. Soon it became only Alex understanding Paul's shouts from the front as they went off into their plans for Glastonbury. As they talked I lay back on the sofa-seat staring at the Nictane poster on the wall of the van, thinking about birds, festivals and, yeah what the summer had in store for me I suppose.

I remember the usual hissing sound from the back of the cooker, which I often took for a small gas leak, was sounding kinda sweet as I held the next drag down. Like a vinyl record as it starts off, and you know what's coming is gonna fucking hit you like a good pint after a long day at work, or a hot shower when you're well cold; or maybe that feeling when you really get into your first cigarette of the morning. A bit like how that intro to the Kews album drifts over you for ages, building up and you know pretty soon the distortion is gonna hit in with the first part of the chorus.

TWO

So Paul or Alex had come up with the idea for us to go over to Thornberry, take a walk to the trigpoint which is like this place where all the families go for their treks at the weekend. By the time we'd got to the entrance at the top of the hill I was feeling pretty wasted.

We got a few looks as the van pulled in to the car park. One guy even telling us to, "Turn the music down," like one minute after we'd stopped; which I couldn't help finding a bit funny actually, you know, how all the families out for their weekend stroll must've viewed us. Even so I kinda kept my amusement to myself 'cause Paul was already going off on one about how people were always treating him like this just 'cause he was different from, "The fucked up expectations of our society," and all that.

So yeah, we were gonna roll a few up first, but with there being too many people around and too fucking hot to be sitting in the van with the door closed we took the gear with us. Alex grabbed his stereo too, whacking on a bit of Ray Zachia as we headed across the gravel to the entrance.

One father made some comment about, "Those hippies, listening to nigger music," as we approached the gate, which really pissed Paul off again. Although instead of saying anything back Alex simply turned the stereo up louder, us all kinda swaggering past, using all the effort in the world to keep ourselves looking serious and then we cracked up once we'd got through and out of sight.

It didn't take us long to get to the trigpoint. Once there though it was pretty crowded so we couldn't roll up as planned. Not that it really mattered to me 'cause I was feeling stoned enough already but for Alex and Paul this was more of an issue – Alex was telling Paul to, "Just skin up." He was all like, "Go on, nobody's gonna do anything," and, "What do you think's gonna happen?" but Paul wasn't having any of it.

While they were arguing over where they were gonna roll the next one I remember entertaining myself by watching all the people as they went past, imagining what their lives were like, why they were there, what their stories were, if they were happy or depressed and stuff. The trigpoint at Thornberry is one of those big ones aimed at places as far away as the other side of the world, like New Zealand and Canada I think. Big enough to sit on which is what we were doing; I guess stopping people from having a proper look, although no one said anything to us or anything.

So after we'd smoked a couple of fags and I'd stared at enough of the passers by, Alex decided we should sit right on the white horse and roll another joint there; us agreeing it was a cool idea.

Despite it being hot Paul was still wearing his fur jacket which I remember 'cause it got caught on the fence on the way over, making this tear right down the inside and all this white fluff was spewing out all over the place. For some reason I really wanted to laugh but neither of them were laughing about it so I kept it in, concentrating on the view in front of me instead as I slid down the slope using my hands as brakes. It was kinda awesome actually, well good to look at. Pretty much your average sight of a patchwork of fields, cows and sheep the size of dots and the odd spec of a person, but with the Amular River looking like a tiny trickle of water with the cliffs in the background it was well impressive.

At first we weren't gonna sit actually on the horse 'cause of getting chalk on our arses but after Alex sat down I guess me and Paul thought, "Fuck it," and joined him. And after moving a couple of stones it was comfortable enough.

After that... well, thinking about it now, we didn't talk much when we were there. It was too hot to do anything but smoke. Although Paul did tell a few Essex-girl jokes which sent us into laughing fits at one point. Also I learnt how to make a simple bong by using an old can we found and putting two holes at the bottom with Alex's pocket-knife.

But that's about it as far as our conversation went. We just lay there feeling the heat as the morning turned to afternoon, listening to Alex's made-up collection of *Music for Summer Drives*.

By the time we were ready to leave it was nearly three o'clock. I'd sort of been keeping an eye on the time from about two but somehow the fact I was starting work at three had been getting more and more insignificant as the afternoon wore on.

We were all sunburnt and sweaty and it took us ages to get back to the top. We were so wasted we could hardly climb the fence. The more difficult we were finding it though, the funnier things became. And later along the path I was kinda swaying into the trees, the others laughing and taking the piss and it was well funny.

By then though a little bit of panic had started to flow over me. I remember wondering if maybe I'd got myself into a bit too much of a state: we were all completely fucked. My mouth was feeling pretty dry all of a sudden too and I remember it being really difficult to roll a fag.

Paul drove as fast as he could manage but he was so wasted. We were going about sixty in a thirty zone and he kept leaning the van into the centre of the road and veering back at the last minute to avoid hitting the oncoming traffic – Alex was finding this pretty funny but I was too involved in working out how I was gonna make it through my shift to pay much attention.

We had to stop off at my house first to get my uniform. Yeah, I remember realising at the last minute that my mum would be back by then and I was telling Paul to park up the road but Alex started taking the piss saying I was embarrassed of my friends. So in the end we went right up my driveway, with me falling out of the van, stumbling through the front door, trying to be as quick as I could (partly 'cause I was late for work and also 'cause I didn't want my mum to see the state I was in). I just about managed to make it in and out without her noticing.

We pulled up outside Price-Savers about five minutes later, pretty impressive to be honest, and I said, "Cheers," to Alex and Paul before running off across the car park.

I rushed in through the back doors, tripping unfortunately on a till bar and setting the alarm off but hurried on without looking back to see if any of the check-out-bitches had noticed it was me. As I carried on down the aisle I remember I was forcing my face into a serious expression but it kept going back into a smile.

When I got to the locker room though, everything seemed a bit less funny. I suddenly felt well tired, really not in the mood for six hours of work.

Then Bradby came in. He told me he'd seen Paul's van through the windows as it was leaving the car park and had come to find me fearing the worst. Taking one look at me he at once seemed to understand what'd been going on.

I met his eyes, which were giving me this sort of accusing gaze, and although feeling guilty I burst into uncontrollable laughter.

I started whispering to him, saying I was, "Really stoned," asking him, "What am I gonna do?" and then I started laughing again, feeling the whole situation was really hilarious I guess, with Bradby totally not amused. He warned me I'd better sort myself out before starting work, then stormed away saying, "You're fucking crazy Chambers," slamming the door shut behind him.

I felt I couldn't start work straight away in the state I was in so I locked myself in the toilet cubicle and sat there for a while trying to shit. I was feeling so bad, but I kept telling myself if I could get through my shift then it'd be like this comical story to say to everyone later.

When I'd finally sorted myself out (water on the face, chewing gum in the mouth) I went off to start work. And once I got onto the produce section I was feeling a bit better, more comfortable; although still a bit nervous of how late I was.

Rather than heading to the shop floor straight away I decided to stay out back, sort some of the potato sacks. If one of the managers questioned me about being late I figured I could always tell them I'd been there the whole time.

When Bradby and Neale found me I was asleep on the potatoes board.

THREE

They woke me up laughing, asking what I'd been doing. Neale said, "Fucking classic," while Bradby looked kinda concerned (I swear I could see a hint of a smile this time though), saying Vader was searching for me and was, "On the war-path." He told me I'd better get on the shop floor to start, "Doing some fucking work," and how there was an L-shape already loaded in the chiller.

I looked up at them saying, "Man, I'm so wasted," and laughed a bit, although not too much 'cause I felt slightly scared of what Bradby had said about Vader. I asked if he or The Terminator knew how late I was, with them both replying, "No," and that I'd been, "Lucky so far."

So Bradby and Neale disappeared and there I was by myself again, walking into the chiller to find it pretty packed, Bradby's L-shape sitting there at the front, full of all the little shit stuff like passion fruit and lychee and was probably only still in there 'cause everyone had been avoiding it – yeah, just as I was about to push the L-shape through the plastic I suddenly thought, "Fuck it," (like, how the hell was I gonna get though it? My head was all spinning and that) and grabbed a salad roller instead; which I knew would probably need doing 'cause no one usually bothered going through salads a second time.

The shop floor was well busy; this much was apparent straight away; tonnes of people. As soon as I got out there (like, immediately) some customer was already asking me for more potatoes 'cause the ones on the section weren't big enough and she wanted to use them for jacket potatoes with chilli or something, but I told her we didn't have any more and carried on going.

Produce was blitzed, although salads weren't too bad. Of course I did get the odd customer studying the roller, looking for stuff not on display but this was pretty normal and to be expected; so I didn't really care.

So I started on the salads, no one really bothering me with anything other than yes/no questions (which were the easiest

– "No,") and I began to feel okay until some old lady came up asking if I was, "Putting out any more button mushrooms," which for some reason started my head spinning; dunno why. I guess 'cause we probably didn't have any and from her expression I knew she wasn't gonna accept this as an answer – she was all like eyeballing me, waiting for a decent response; which I didn't really have.

I looked across at Neale who was working a bananas roller on the other side of the section and thought about asking him but instead stupidly decided there was no reason I couldn't deal with this myself; how it'd be a good step in adjusting to being at work. So I asked her to say again what sort of mushrooms she wanted and then for some reason came out with this stuff about how shitake mushrooms were, "Actually okay to use in a lot of dishes." (I guess thinking about it now I felt this nice old lady would at least appreciate a bit of conversation with a bright young student; but she was merely staring at me as if I was mad).

I continued, asking, "What do you want the mushrooms for?" but before she could answer Bradby appeared out of nowhere telling her, "We'll have a look out the back," and then was guiding me away with him back towards the warehouse.

A bit later on I was beginning to seriously consider going home, saying I was sick or something when Neale spotted me from the other end of the aisle, started laughing and then walked off, probably to tell someone about the state I was in. And it was then I decided it might be more fun to stay at work. Like, I remember thinking if I could find a place to simply get on with something and make it through the day, I could tell everyone about it later and it'd be funny.

I'd been hiding behind a stack of chicken sauce at the time 'cause I'd seen Hitler coming and had been trying to make up my mind whether to avoid him or walk up saying I was sick. My new plan was to find a safe place quick where no one could bother me so I headed back to the warehouse armed with the excuse of a customer asking me for skimmed milk, which I knew we'd run out of.

Hitler caught me as I was walking past the deli; I guess he'd been watching me the whole time. He asked who else was on my department, a question I should've seen coming, and I replied, "Bradby and Neale," without thinking.

He studied me for a moment, making me feel pretty nervous. I remember wondering if he knew I was stoned 'cause maybe someone had said something to him about me or something, but finally all he came out with was, "I'd like you to help on provisions."

So I was putting yoghurts out for most of the afternoon; not so bad. I mean I thought it best to get on with my work, avoid any managers until my head cleared up. My stomach was feeling pretty weird as well; I needed something to take my mind off any potential throwing up incidents. I passed the time away singing the whole Nictane album in my head, like properly from start to finish. And by the time supper break came round I was back to feeling okay.

When I got to the canteen there were only cheese sandwiches left in the vending machine but I got a Fry's Turkish Delight to go with them and a coffee.

Bradby was in there looking at some piece of paper The Terminator had given him so I sat on the same table. He asked what I was doing that night as I sat down, if I was going out in Bracksea to which I replied how I'd probably head down The Bowman and he was like, "Cool," and how he might be down there. Yeah I remember also saying I was feeling a bit better, with him giving me a, "Don't worry about it," and that he'd been a bit stressed with all the, "Shit they've been putting on me this month."

In the smoking room I chatted to Sereme for a bit. She came in with her long legs and big eyes, moaning about the work, looking at me with that expression she always gave me, like an, "Oh I so want you Chambers, when are you gonna make the first move?" sort of thing but I knew not to read too much into it. We talked a little about college, after which I gave her the low-down on my afternoon, pretending to be really enthusiastic about my Turkish Delight, making her laugh.

So pretty soon it was seven o'clock and I was by myself having been given the task of finishing yoghurts and fats before I went home.

It took me ages to dress it all. I tried singing to make the time go quicker but it didn't work this time 'cause I'd started thinking about Colin again, what he'd said to me the last time I'd seen him – and you know how hard it is to stop mulling over something you don't wanna think about once you've started. Like trying to get a song out your head when you've been stuck with it all day going round and round, again and again until you're ready to kill yourself.

FOUR

I got out of work half an hour early 'cause there were no managers around to stop me. Before I knew it I was standing outside Duncan's flat, banging on his window, hoping to hell he hadn't already left. I was out there for ages too, standing around wondering whether to go to the extreme of shouting through the letterbox until finally Duncan came out; looking pretty sober actually.

He was like, "Up for a good night?" All enthusiastic and that, which I knew meant he was obviously in one of his turn-over-a-new-leaf moods: always shit to, I dunno, *put up with* or whatever. So yeah, I tried not to encourage him too much on the way there, give him a chance to talk, so I told him the story about my day, how stoned I'd been, how I'd even fallen asleep at work; although of course he didn't find it as funny as he usually would've.

We got down The Bowman at about nine. Neale was already there with Graz, sitting at one of the round tables by the fruit machines. Me and Duncan said, "Hi," and then went to get some in.

At the bar Ambra spotted us straight away, serving us with some beers and four free chasers (these little blue drinks which tasted like shit but were well strong). She was looking pretty hot as usual, this time wearing a light green flowery dress over jeans, with her hair in pigtails which, I don't know why but that really used to do it for me; the pigtails I mean. I didn't have the chance to talk to her much though 'cause she was busy; but she did ask what I was planning to do once the summer was over as she took the money – I said I wasn't sure and she told me she was gonna go travelling, which sounded quite cool: although when I asked her, "Where?" she just said, "All over."

When we got back to the table Neale and Graz were talking to a couple of birds who I think were in Graz's year but they left when we arrived; though not 'cause of us or anything.

The place was totally busy already, full of the usual Friday night crowd, all pissed, shouting and having a good time.

And I remember I felt well happy to be in there at that moment, totally grateful for Graz, Neale and Duncan's… just being there I guess.

Anyway, as I sat down Graz asked me if I'd heard the new Pearls single (which was shit) and we argued about that for a while – fucking Pearls: bunch of scene-stars trying to sound like The Crushed and Hessian. Graz thought they were so good though. He was describing it as the, "Perfect song for the summer."

Neale was looking kinda smug, not surprising considering his latest pull. After arguing with Graz I asked Neale if his new bird was joining us later, him saying, "Maybe," and looking like he didn't wanna go into any more detail so of course we all started pushing him to tell us all about her.

So it was a good start, that night. Usually it took a few for us to get going, but what with the day I'd had and Neale's new found status we had plenty to talk about.

Ambra came over to our table after a while, flirting with Graz, then talking to Duncan about travelling, really starting him off on his whole new-leaf thing – He was all, "I'm gonna do it, I'm gonna save so much money from not smoking pot that I'll have enough to go to Australia," and was all calculating money and stuff.

A few pints later when everything around us was starting to get that little bit more blurred and everything and everyone seemed to be moving that little bit faster we decided to head off down The Temple.

*

We'd made the choice of going to The Temple rather than straight to 85s 'cause Duncan said his brother was down there and wanted to catch up with him. Not that we were totally against the idea or anything. Although on the way there Neale was complaining about the place, how it was full of, "Old druggies," and all the fag burns in the carpets and the fact the pool tables sloped to one side; how there was never anywhere to sit. But we just told him to shut up 'cause he was ginger and therefore what he thought didn't count for anything.

Anyway, the bouncers were pretty lenient for once that night, not even bothering to ask any questions – even to Graz who'd just got his hair cut and was looking about twelve – so we had no problems getting in.

As soon as we got through the doors Duncan spotted a couple of his brother's mates and went off to talk to them, while Graz and Neale headed to the bar. I decided to go through to the back to look for Colin, who I found playing pool with one of his new townie mates.

When he saw me he was all like, "Hey Chambers, how's it going?" Not a hint of what he'd said the last time I'd seen him or anything.

I asked how long he'd been down there, him replying, "Not that long," then kinda went back to concentrating on the game.

Graz came through at that point, showing me this huge whisky he'd got us, which tasted well strong, saying Neale and Duncan were talking to some people Duncan knew from his work, and, "Do ya wanna go join them?" but I shouted, "No."

I stood there for a while looking at Colin, not saying much to either him or Graz actually, before I finally started a conversation with Graz about the Patterson song that was playing, which was really cool; although Graz wasn't totally convinced.

I rolled a cigarette, half listening to Graz, half watching Colin playing pool and then I was scanning the place, looking for anyone I could recognise amongst all the people in there; without much luck.

I did spot a semi-fit girl though, sitting by herself on one of the chairs by the old stage at the end of the room and thought for a while about going over to talk to her. She was wearing this orange dress that really showed off her tits, made of the material which just kinda like shines if you know what I mean. Like the one that looks like silk but probably isn't. And it was well hard to keep myself from staring.

15

As I sparked up Graz began a half hearted conversation about college but I wasn't really listening and I think he could tell 'cause before long he asked if I wanted to sit in the corner on the floor, our usual spot in The Temple for watching the crowd and listening to the tunes.

Colin was beating everybody on the pool table: the winner-stays-on rule doing pretty well for him. And at one point I noticed he started putting this other guy's balls in the table just to take the piss and then, when the guy finally got angry, Colin pushed him into the wall and the guy hit his head; there was even blood on the wall – kinda funny in a weird sort of way, and I think we were all laughing…

Anyway, then Charlotte came over to talk to Graz so I went for a piss to leave them to it. I still had a bit of a thing for her you see, but I knew it was Graz she was interested in. I was sure he still had a soft spot for her too, despite of what he'd said about her being a, "Fat slag," whenever we were pushing him about it.

It was quiet in the bogs, making me feel both sober and drunk at the same time if you know what I mean. One of the Temple locals tried to talk to me when I was in there. He was like, "Having a good night?" and I was like, "Yeah, pretty good," but that was it.

When I got out Charlotte had gone. I gestured to Graz to see if he wanted another drink and he nodded, shouting, "Get the *house* whisky."

*

There was a different atmosphere out the front. Loads of people, most of them older than me. And it was noisier too. There was a karaoke thing starting up and it was all like mad and crazy.

I looked around for Duncan and Neale but they didn't seem to be anywhere. So I queued up for the drinks by myself, feeling a bit awkward actually, like a bit more wary of pushing my way to the bar as I usually would've done. And once I'd finally got there it was well difficult to get served

16

'cause there were so many other people fighting for drinks.

Finally one of the bar staff noticed me though, I think 'cause I'd obviously been there for so long, and I shouted to her what I wanted. It was double for 50p extra for the house whisky so I got me and Graz and Colin a couple each. I told the barmaid I wanted them in three glasses and it took her ages to understand what I meant.

While I was waiting for them the girl in the orange dress, who I'd been staring at before, appeared next to me out of nowhere – actually I dunno how long she'd been there to be honest. But anyway she was sort of pushing her arse into mine and I felt like I should say something so I leaned into her and tried to make eye contact. I think I just said, "All right?" but whatever it was she gave me a questioning look, then kinda scowled at me sarcastically when I failed to say anything back. So I gave it one more try with a, "What?" combined with a cheeky smile but she wasn't having any of it. (She did have well nice tits though; and I got a good look).

Colin was still playing pool when I got back and not really sure where to put his drink I placed it on the pool table; after his shot he said, "Cheers," and downed it.

Graz was in the corner of the room, carefully rolling a one skin (tongue hanging out, looking like, I dunno, a kid with a new toy or whatever) not really appreciating the sudden attention when I shouted to ask if he wanted to put on some better tunes. He quickly said for me to, "Wait a minute," but I couldn't be arsed so I went over there by myself.

At the jukebox I looked for the Celebrations album from which I selected a couple of songs; then put on *It's up To You When You Want* 'cause I knew Graz would appreciate it, afterwards choosing *Component 2* by Planquez which is always a good tune to hear, and finally I fancied picking something a bit more alternative so I decided on the secret track from the new Kews album which I reckoned would weird a few people out.

The joint was only a one-skin and not particularly strong but after a few drags me and Graz really started to notice the music and were singing away. I told him about the girl at the bar, how she'd been rude to me, although instead of finding it funny he said I should, "Just go for it."

I looked over at Colin again who was now completely taking the piss out of the guy he was playing. Like really badly. And he was doing all these trick shots, closing his eyes and stuff.

I remember it was kinda funny to see him prancing around the table, getting so into it, looking so happy. But something about it also seemed a bit wrong. Like for some reason I totally wanted him to stop and come sit with us.

When I shouted to ask if he wanted another drink though, he either didn't hear or was just ignoring me. So I asked Graz if he was up for another whisky, and turned my thoughts back to orange-dress-girl.

FIVE

So this time it was a Sunday, about a week and a half later, maybe two weeks. And apart from seeing Colin's actions on the pool table nothing that weird had really happened to me yet. All in all you could say I was feeling pretty normal still.

It was around eleven o'clock. I was on my way to Duncan's, late 'cause of The Terminator wanting me to close up produce so I'd had to finish at ten. Everyone was already there when I arrived, all watching *The Sarsaparilla*; the flat looking like a tip again.

Duncan sat back in his usual place on the floor by the TV and started rolling a cigarette. Bradby mumbled "Alright?" and I responded, "Alright," back. No one else said anything. All just watching the film, obviously stoned.

I looked for somewhere to sit, feeling a bit pissed off 'cause I'd been hoping for a proper chance to have a good night and was in the mood to talk – it was already becoming obvious I wasn't gonna get any good conversation for a while. So yeah, instead of sitting down immediately I asked if anyone wanted tea, to which everyone was like, "Yeah!" (That is except Neale's girlfriend who didn't want anything, Ambra who wanted water, and Sereme needed a coffee predictably but whatever).

Once in the kitchen I looked around for mugs, finding two in the cupboard, one on the table; which was dirty and needed washing, and a few in the sink full of murky water with old tea bags. I returned to the front room searching for anything cleaner, and like maybe a glass or something for Ambra's water; discovering one on the floor next to Duncan.

My eyes drifted towards the film for a while. It was at the part where the Casio-tone song's playing and The Triple's are all dancing in the café – a cool scene to watch, however many times you've seen it. The part when you first realise the guy with one eye is interested in Karen but you're still not sure if it's him who's been sending her the letters and it's all intense and stuff.

Everyone was well into it and didn't seem to be noticing

me. I remember Graz laying on the floor the other side of the TV with Sereme. Bradby, Neale and his girlfriend were on the sofa. Ambra had the armchair and Charlotte was on the wicker-chair by the window.

I stood there considering the best place to sit later. It seemed like a choice between the floor or maybe squeezing onto the sofa next to Neale's girlfriend or Bradby.

The music from the film stopped and it went back to a boring part so I checked for any more cups (so I didn't have to wash the ones in the sink), then searched for any sign of gear lying around but couldn't see either. So I went again to the kitchen, put on the radio and rolled a fag before starting the washing up.

*

Sereme had her arm round Graz when I came back with the drinks. I didn't feel like sitting on the floor next to them so I went over to the sofa asking everyone to budge up. Rather than having my leg touching Bradby's for the rest of the night I figured it'd be better to go straight for the other side next to Neale's girlfriend. If I was gonna be squashed up to someone I remember thinking I'd rather it be a girl – although as I sat down I did sense a bit of amusement from the others. And as Neale's girlfriend moved towards Neale I wasn't sure if it was a case of her moving closer to him or further away from me; but I didn't care.

I sat back with my tea, not really interested in the film and gazed around wondering when someone was gonna roll another joint: everything was completely silent though, everyone just gawking at the TV.

The film was now at the part where Karen is driving up to the house at the top of the mountain. All the camera angles are all over the place with the section in black and white to make it all seem as if it's a dream or something. It is sort of a cool part actually, but all I could honestly think about was, *"When's somebody gonna roll another joint for fuck's sake so I can actually appreciate this at least?"*

I stared at the cat picture for a bit; then the lava lamp by the wicker chair caught my attention for a while as normal. All in all though I must admit I was kinda bored.

Finally when I'd given up waiting I said, "Does anyone want me to skin up?" and like immediately some weed and king-skins flew over from Duncan, who said, "Ok, roll up you fucking cane-head," before looking back at the film – I realised then how it must've been obvious what I was thinking and felt a bit guilty actually; but not that much.

I ripped out three skins, which were stuck together a bit but all right. And there was plenty of gear so I decided I was gonna pack this one to give myself the chance to catch up. Everyone did seem pretty far gone. And the smell of weed in the room was well strong.

I started rolling up while looking around at everybody again – then caught Charlotte staring at me and I remember not being sure whether she wanted to talk or was simply hoping I'd pass it her way first: but when I met her eye she looked away quickly.

The joint was quite difficult to roll 'cause of the papers not having much stick on them and I had to lick it loads of times once I'd finished. After I'd given it enough time to dry though and been bored for long enough I took my first drag and it felt pretty good. A couple more drags held down and suddenly I was in the room.

So, before long I started to notice how awkward Charlotte was looking. She was just sitting there dressed up in her like, *clubbers' uniform*, playing with the remains of her tea, looking like, I dunno, like she just didn't belong if you know what I mean… And yeah, the more I watched her the more it really started to disturb me. When I passed her the joint she smiled and said, "No thanks," and seemed a bit pissed off. For a minute she sort of glanced at me as if she was gonna say something but didn't.

At this point Graz suddenly came up for air, pushing Sereme off him saying, "I'll have some of that," and grabbed the joint off me. As he took it I asked if he was still up for going to the next indie night down the Basement with him

21

replying, "For sure!"

A couple of murmurs followed but this was all; I guess everyone was still too engrossed with the film to say much. And after the joint (which never came back round again) had finished and the film still hadn't I was feeling stoned enough but nonetheless bored so I said I was, "Gonna go for a walk down the offie," and asked if anyone wanted anything. No one responded apart from Charlotte who said she'd join me. I hadn't really bargained on any company, especially from Charlotte who I didn't know that well but I thought, "Fuck it," and said, "Cool."

It was well cold once we'd got outside. Charlotte had a coat – one of those long duffle coats which are really warm; although she seemed to be wearing it more for style than anything else and didn't do it up – but I had fuck all to keep me from freezing. I did think about going back to see if I could borrow something from Duncan but then thought "Fuck it," and instead blagged one of Charlotte's menthols to keep me going.

I let her do the talking at the start. She made some comments about the weather and then asked if I knew what I wanted to do once the summer was over, me saying I didn't really know or care. Following this she asked if there were any girls I was interested in, which I knew she would 'cause people were always asking me that, so I kept my answer short and said, "Do you know any?" which I thought was quite a cool response but she didn't laugh or say anything.

We were almost in town when she brought up the subject of Colin, saying, "Did you know he had a problem?" or something like this and, yeah, at the time I wondered if she was talking about the incident by the pool tables in The Temple, kinda taking me by surprise to be honest with me not really knowing what to say. I wasn't completely sure what the hell she was talking about actually.

I said, "What do you mean?" which I regretted immediately 'cause as she looked back at me all sympathetically, I kinda felt a bit sick all of a sudden. It was, I dunno, like when you're well stoned and get home and see your mum, it's okay until sometimes she starts looking at you funny and then you feel a bit sick so you say you're a little drunk and go up to your room and feel better once you're up there. That's what I felt. Like, I wanted to not have her staring at me, analysing my expression.

I remember trying to think of what I could use to get out of this sudden interrogation but all I ended up saying again was, "I dunno, what you mean?"

She was like, "Do you think he's happy?"

And I said, "Who is?"

Then she was asking me what he was doing that night or something and when I said that I didn't know she said, "How come? You guys were always together," but I didn't answer her.

When we got to the off license though, everything was all right again. I'd had another cigarette and Charlotte had changed the subject, talking for ages about her new job at the bank, not seeming to have noticed the fact I'd been pissed off with her before.

The sight of all the alcohol had made me forget all of that shit too as I wandered round the place trying to decide what to buy. I started on the wines, looking to see if I could find the cheapest, then went back to Charlotte, asking what she thought about wine and whether she liked it. Then before she could answer I'd changed my mind and gone over to the beers trying to work out which was the best offer, staring at them for ages until I finally realised I'd been staring for a bit too long. I turned around to see what Charlotte was looking at, but she was just looking at me.

She said, "Shall we just get some vodka and a couple of bottles of hooch?" so we did. And at the counter I got some malteasers too, but this was all 'cause I didn't wanna go over the top 'cause of Charlotte being there (even though I was suddenly feeling pretty hungry).

Once we got outside with all the stuff in the bag I must admit I felt a bit disappointed to be going back to Duncan's. I started thinking how it might be cool to open up the vodka, maybe take a walk and find somewhere to drink, just the two of us. Before I had the chance to share my idea Charlotte turned to me coming out with, "Shall we head up the park? Drink some of the vodka first?" and I said, "Cool."

Then, still looking at me she said, "That film was so boring," and I laughed and said, "It's okay, but I know what you mean," telling her I was expecting the night to be a bit more like a party, with her replying, "Me too!" all enthusiastically. And then we were laughing at the same time.

*

So we headed up the park and now I felt more like talking. We chatted quite a bit on the way up there, this time the conversation being a lot easier to handle: just bullshit stuff I think; although I do remember asking Charlotte if she'd anyone she was interested in and she looked at me, kinda scowling and said, "As if you don't know." I straight away knew she meant Graz, realising all of a sudden why she'd probably been so keen to get away from Duncan's flat – I wondered who'd exactly invited her there in the first place and if it'd been Graz. (Duncan didn't really invite people over, they just showed up).

So there we were cutting into the park through the alleyway behind Hammond Street, drinking vodka along the way; talking about how shit Bracksea was.

We got out into the open to discover some townie kids there, a bit younger than us, pissing about on the swings so we went and sat on the roundabout. I rolled a cigarette and had a bit more vodka; Charlotte opened up one of the bottles of hooch.

It was only a short time before the townies started calling over to us saying, "Are you gonna shag her mate!" and stuff like this. Charlotte was cool though. Somehow I felt safe with her even though I didn't know her so well. I knew she could outdo anyone in the whole taking-the-piss game 'cause I'd seen her in action enough times. I remember once some Skipton lads were trying it on and she obviously wasn't in the mood, telling them to, "Piss off." When one of them made the mistake of saying she was a, "Fat bitch anyway," it was like, *man you're so gonna regret that* – by the time Charlotte had finished with him he was almost crying.

I got pissed quite quickly actually, probably 'cause I hadn't eaten. I can't remember much about our conversation but I know it was basically aimed towards how funny it was to be young or how cool it was gonna be when we got older; or maybe how shit it was gonna be: whatever it was it was well comical.

After a bit I lay back on the roundabout, not feeling the need to talk any more. I remember imagining if Orion wasn't a hunter with a bow and arrow but was like a stoner with a big fat joint. It was kinda amusing and I started laughing. Then out of nowhere Charlotte leaned over began kissing me.

Her hair was in my face, her cleavage so big and I remember thinking how good it'd be to get her tits out; but for some reason I rolled away, grabbed one of the bottles of hooch and proceeded to open the top of it with my teeth; like trying to act cool as if nothing had happened.

Charlotte didn't do anything, she just watched me. Then, I dunno, for some reason I started thinking about Colin again and my head started spinning. I looked towards Charlotte and her face was all a blur, mouthing some words to me I couldn't hear before everything went black.

SIX

I'd either fainted or totally zoned out completely for I dunno how long. When I came to, Charlotte had lit another cigarette.

I looked around trying to work out what the fuck had just happened; all I could think was how the fire on the end of Charlotte's cigarette was looking so much bigger than all the stars in the sky behind her; and how much this just wasn't making any sense.

I sat up, sorting my head with a couple more swigs of vodka and I guess we shared quite a few minutes of silence, although nothing was awkward; it could've lasted forever as far as I was concerned.

Finally Charlotte broke the peace though and started talking about Graz again, how much she liked him and *what the hell did he see in Sereme anyway?* Going off on one about how Sereme thought she was, "So fucking special," and stuff.

It's weird 'cause my head was killing me and she was going on and on but, I dunno, I suddenly really liked Charlotte at that moment; dunno why. I just remember this moment of noticing how the skin on her face was flaky up close, her hair kinda dry and stiff in places and it gradually becoming obvious how her hair colour wasn't natural but... well, there was something about her that was kinda warm.

So I told her to forget about Graz who was, "A slag," anyway, how she could do better and said, "Who the fuck invites a girl out, who he knows is into him, and then gets off with another girl right in front of her for the whole fucking night?"

Charlotte looked a bit shocked at first and I wondered if I'd gone too far but after she'd taken a long drag on her cigarette she looked back at me, right into my eyes and I got this weird feeling she liked me too.

It was then when I nearly said it was okay to ask about Colin again and that I was sorry. But deciding one crazy outburst was enough, I left it.

26

Pretty soon she was giving me a hug which was well nice actually. She felt soft and warm, a proper hug, not one of those half-arsed friendship hugs girls usually give you. Even so, as her tits pressed up against me it wasn't long before I began to get a hard on so I quickly patted her on the back and let go.

I said we'd better be getting back 'cause the others would be wondering where we were; with her saying how they probably weren't: well she actually said, "Do you really think so?" but I got her meaning.

SEVEN

Charlotte didn't come with me back to the flat. She told me she couldn't be bothered and lived near the park anyway so I left alone.

It was a bit scary actually, walking by myself and all, and I wished I had my walkman; I remember feeling it would've been a lot better to be listening to some tunes.

I didn't swig the vodka 'cause I was feeling quite pissed and having trouble walking in a straight line. And then I started getting a bit of a headache again after I'd taken a piss in the alleyway. But I finished the hooch and had another menthol, which I'd blagged from Charlotte before we'd parted.

When I got to the flat Bradby, Neale and his girlfriend had gone, and Sereme had fucked off too which I was a bit surprised about. The three of them (Graz, Duncan and Ambra) were having a chill-out session; the *No Reconciliations* album was playing. All of them teased me about Charlotte as soon as I walked in, with an, "Ahhhh, Chambers you sly dog," sort of thing, which was weird 'cause they didn't even know what'd gone on and I remember thinking just 'cause we went for a walk it didn't mean anything, which is what I said.

It was good to be back though, and warm and this time Duncan offered to make me a tea.

We played the spoons game for a bit which was well funny, Duncan doing his usual thing with the drumsticks. Then I remembered about the malteasers in my pocket and it was like, "Fucking result!"

Towards the end of the night we started talking about our college ball, what we'd thought of it 'cause Ambra started us off by saying the guy she was now seeing was the guy she'd met at the college ball who didn't actually go to our college at all, was twenty-three and had been someone's mate or brother, or both. None of us could actually remember seeing her there though and we were teasing her, saying how, was she sure that she'd actually gone to the right party? How maybe *she'd* been the one in the wrong place.

So we all talked about that night for a while. How we'd gotten really drunk at the bar on Bradby's tequila shots, how there'd been this rumour that Tom Michaels from Hessian was gonna be there; Graz admitted he'd been kinda looking forward to seeing him, which made us all totally crack up.

Duncan reminded us about Colin breaking the DJ's Trendy Holmes record to stop him playing it. I said how I'd thought I was gonna pull the blue-haired girl from Skipton until she'd finally ditched me for some townie twat, with Graz saying, "That was the guy who always used to piss his pants in primary school," and we all had a laugh about that. Duncan (yeah, I think that was his third college ball) was going on about the weed he'd got from Amsterdam especially for the night which had got us completely fucked on the rugby pitch once everyone else had gone home.

I started to think about us all there under the stars, like how cool everything had been at that moment, with the night having been such a good one, how we were all still mates after surviving however many years of school and college together.

I guess this was when I realised I had to see Colin again and talk to him.

Before too long after I said I had to piss off, and Ambra said, "I'd better be leaving too." Duncan offered one more joint for the road, Graz of course giving a, "Yeah, why not?" but I really had to get going so I didn't say anything.

Ambra took fucking ages to get ready. She was all saying bullshit stuff like, "Bye," and, "Thanks for the night," suddenly talking more to Graz and Duncan about nothing of any significance. I stood outside waiting for her 'cause I didn't wanna just walk off and was kinda hopping from one foot to the other to stay warm before she finally got her shit together and came out.

When she got outside though she just smiled and said, "See you," and that was it; which annoyed me a bit, although we were both stoned so I didn't really care.

I couldn't really phone Colin 'cause it was late. Once

29

Ambra had gone I half considered using the phone box to call his house but then figured if he wasn't round Duncan's then he'd probably be up by the cliffs so I headed there.

I went the beach way, passing town, cut through the golf course and walked up the path leading to the car park. When I got to the top I carried on down towards the coast guard cottages but instead of turning left to the other side of the hill that leads to the beach I went up past the line of gorse bushes, over to the fence by the edge. Once I got to the fence I sat down and waited.

I rolled another fag while I sat there. It was really windy all of a sudden; I hoped it wouldn't be too long a wait.

I looked back a few times along the path I'd taken. I was feeling a bit paranoid to be honest about seeing someone around. But also I wanted to make sure I'd notice when Colin was coming towards me. This was 'cause I wanted to have time to prepare, to think properly about what to say.

There were a couple of times I thought I saw him. Some strange sounds were coming from behind the cottages and later the fence started shaking but on both occasions I reckon it was just the wind 'cause there was a lot of it with me on the cliff edge and all.

And there was one time when I really thought it was him 'cause I heard shouting.

But finally I gave up and made my way back down again.

When I got to the town everything was totally quiet, kinda eerie rather than relaxing. I remember walking to my house as fast as I could.

My bed felt well nice when I got home and I went to sleep pretty quickly. I dreamt about being up on the cliffs, finding Colin on the cliff edge where I'd been sitting and I was trying to wake him up but he just wasn't moving. And then later I had the same dream except this time I woke him up and when his eyes opened he looked at me saying, "Why didn't you come back for me Chambers?" and sort of got up, pushing me a couple of times before I finally fell over. Then he turned to the cliff, ran and jumped off.

I woke up after each dream but didn't feel frightened. I

merely felt well happy I wasn't still out in the cold, satisfied with going back to sleep in my warm bed.

EIGHT

There was this one time me and Colin were stuck in detention after school, sitting in the biology lab, just the two of us – yeah, Mr. Andrews had kept us back 'cause we'd been caught looking at snot under the microscope which we thought was pretty funny at the time.

We were sitting in the empty classroom on the desks at the back by the windows when Colin suddenly turned to me saying all about how one day he wanted to be a teacher; going off on one as he sometimes did, all animated and that, but with this really serious look in his eyes. I remember him all filled with enthusiasm and it being a bit weird actually. Like how at first I wasn't sure how to take him but listening anyway as he went on about how he really thought he could be good at it. How he reckoned it'd be, "Cool to do something worthwhile," and could really make a difference by simply not being, "An arse-hole."

I dunno where it came from or why he chose to tell me in this sudden outburst, or at that particular moment (this was the only time he ever mentioned it), but, actually, now I consider it, I reckon it would've been cool him being a teacher. There was something about Colin which was kind of, I dunno, just the way that when he spoke everyone listened.

Anyway, yeah, not a lot of people knew this about Colin. His serious side I mean. The fact he actually, I dunno, how he actually did wanna do something with his life.

NINE

What I'm gonna talk about next is the day I awoke with the fizzing sound in my head. This may well have been only a night or two after I'd gone up to the cliffs looking for Colin. There again maybe it was longer. It's kinda hard to tell now. Although as far as I'm concerned there wasn't much time in between; at least as my memory goes. And if anything did happen that I've missed I guess it's irrelevant.

So yeah, I woke up and there was this fizzing sound in my head. Like, I dunno, similar to the white noise when the radio is tuned between stations if you know what I mean. Except a bit nastier, like a bad sound effect from a horror movie; faint, but enough to be annoying.

I remember ignoring it at first, thinking it was only earache and how it'd go away before too long. But I had a shower and cleaned my ears with cotton buds, letting all the water go in, yawned about a hundred times; then as I got out the bathroom I had the new idea of it not being me but something in the house so I was going in all the rooms to see where the sound was the loudest.

I actually went in my mum's room first 'cause it's next to the bathroom; although I didn't stay in there for long. Just had a quick scan around, going to the window and back to see if I could notice any change in like the pitch or strength of the noise but there was no obvious difference.

I checked the smoke alarm on the landing to see if the batteries were okay and they seemed to be all right. And I went downstairs to test the other smoke alarm in the hall which had no problems either.

I also had a good root around the front room 'cause there's loads of shit in there – well, not now but there was for a long time. My mum's junk, accumulated over the years: mostly ornaments and papers from her art classes; nothing which could really have been the source, though I figured maybe there was some kind of dying electrical device buried somewhere amongst the crap.

Next I headed to the kitchen which… yeah, at the time the

kitchen was no better as far as junk's concerned so there were plenty of possibilities in there too. But there was nothing so I gave up after this.

To be honest as in my mum's room I hadn't noticed any difference in sound (like the pitch, strength or whatever) when walking around the kitchen or the front room and after a while I guess I wasn't totally expecting to find something. The fizzing really did feel as if it was coming from the inside of my head. I suppose looking for another source merely gave me something to focus on.

Anyway, finally deciding if I stopped thinking about the sound it might go away I put on the radio to see if it'd drown it out or at least take my mind off it; even briefly tuning it to a frequency between stations; although this simply made things worse so I left it on a talk radio show – one of those where people phone to complain about shit with the host winding them up even more and it's supposed to be entertaining.

So there I was, listening to the radio, making my breakfast of toast, jam and a cup of tea. I had a cigarette and a look at one of my mum's magazines, then watched a bit of TV – first in the kitchen, after a while in the front room ('cause the set's bigger in there).

I actually took in a lot of MTV that morning. Now I'm thinking about it I remember putting it on really loud and sitting in the porch puffing away on cigarettes, wishing I had something stronger to smoke – partly 'cause it would've been cool to have a joint, what with the sun, MTV and that. But mostly 'cause the fucking fizzing noise, however faint, just wasn't going away.

TEN

In some ways the fizzing sound isn't totally important. Although my day really did begin like this: sitting in the porch till the morning turned to afternoon, listening to all the shit MTV had to offer, trying to clear my mind and ignore the fizzing. (And I remember watching this cat chasing all the birds in the garden for a while too but I suppose that's not important either).

So there I was wishing I had a joint or beer or something to make the beginnings of my day a bit nicer; the sound still in my mind, still faint, still fucking annoying. My head starting to hurt more and more the longer I sat there baking under the magnified rays of the sun. Me not being arsed enough to move and... well yeah you get the picture. This was my morning.

My mum was due back at around two o'clock so just before then I decided to go out for a walk 'cause I wasn't feeling in the best of moods and really didn't feel like facing the chances of any potential argument.

I went upstairs, put on some jeans, tied my Patterson hoody around my waste, grabbed my wallet and was out the door within a couple of minutes. And it was only after I'd left the house I realised that maybe I should've, or at least could've, phoned someone so at least I'd have some direction to be heading in. But I couldn't be arsed to go back inside so I just carried on down my road towards the corner shop; I needed some more tobacco anyway.

On my way out of the newsagents I remember looking left towards the seafront, wondering if it'd be worth a walk down there, see if anyone I knew was on the beach. I had a feeling there was a good possibility of running into Graz and his mates down there 'cause... yeah me, Graz and Colin used to spend a lot of time down the beach at one point. Still now I always imagine him to be down there whenever I walk past.

But anyway, after coming out newsagents I spotted the pub across the road – High Lanes, which was sort of my local, even though I hardly ever went there – and decided to go

35

over for a drink. It wasn't the sort of thing I usually would've done, go to a pub during the day by myself and all, but in this instance I just thought, "Fuck it, why not?"

The road was a little hazy as I approached the junction. You know, how sometimes the heat affects the way you see things in the summer. Like when cars are far away and they look like they're melting. Also High Lanes is one of those big white pubs on the outside. Big white walls which were kinda hard to look at as I walked towards it. I remember wishing I'd brought my sunglasses.

As soon as I got in the pub I spotted Colin sitting by himself at one of the tables by the windows to the left side of the bar. There was this stream of light coming in through the glass behind him and he had his back to me. His hair was different 'cause, well he'd obviously shaved it all off, and I remember the light from the window was reflecting off his scalp; which looked kinda weird. All the same I recognised him straight away.

I got a drink first rather than go over to say, "Hi," immediately 'cause I didn't wanna seem too like, I dunno, grateful for him being there I suppose. I guess I wanted to play it cool and that.

I asked the barman for a Fosters, who was this middle-aged guy with sweaty hair combed across what was obviously a balding head. He grunted at me in disapproval as though I was some young student type who didn't appreciate real beer or something – I'm not really that much of a beer connoisseur: the Fosters tap was in front of me so I simply asked for that – and took ages 'cause he was in conversation with this old guy sitting at the bar next to me and opposite him; I don't remember what they were talking about. Actually I wasn't listening. I needed time to work out what I was gonna say to Colin.

I reckon there were just four of us in the pub at that point. There was no music playing, the voices of the barman and the old man were like echoing and the noise of my pint being poured was pretty loud.

I remember it was then as I was waiting at the bar that I

noticed the fizzing sound had disappeared. I turned to look at Colin and I swear he was smiling – although I can't be sure 'cause he still had his back to me. But you know how sometimes you can tell when someone's smiling even when you can't see their face.

*

Colin was wearing the same as me. Jeans, a T-shirt, and a hoody was slung over the chair beside him. The T-shirt was different 'cause it was black with red writing on while mine was white with blue writing on (his had *Dave's Communication*; mine simply said, *City Life* in small letters). His hoody was plain white; opposed to my dark red.

I sat opposite him and put my pint down, taking out my backy, waiting for him to say something but he didn't so I started with a "Hey man, how's it going?" and he looked up at me and said, "What do you think?" all sarcastically and that, which was kinda typical of him but it still took me by surprise considering the situation.

Yeah, thinking about it now it was pretty strange looking at Colin with a shaven head for the first time and maybe this also influenced the way I reacted to seeing him.

He looked weird, younger than usual, but in a way older too. And his nose and eyes seemed bigger, sort of like they'd been stuck on his face by someone. Like one of those kids' toys where you stick all the features on to make a face. A face without a body most of the time… yeah… but anyway I then said, "Sorry," which probably wasn't exactly the right thing to say 'cause I really should've just given him some lip. Said like, "What the fuck are you looking at?" or made a joke, but at the time I totally did feel sorry so that's what I said.

Actually this is all a little weird to talk about now. Half 'cause it's kinda hard to tell what happened with any sort of accuracy as to the exact conversation (it's all a bit of a blur), and yeah, half 'cause, well, it's just strange to be thinking about this.

Basically I remember that we made small talk. About college and how shit Bracksea was; usual stuff. I told him about Neale's new girlfriend too, and gave him the low-down on some of the new summer tunes that'd been released since we'd last seen each other.

But I should also mention that a lot of what I said seemed to cause Colin to throw comments back at me with a sort of, I dunno, like bitterness or something. And at the time I remember I wasn't really sure why or for what reason he had to be pissed off with me.

For example when I asked Colin if he was, "Going to The Basement this month?" he said, "What's the fucking point?" And when I said, "I want you to go," he said, "You couldn't give a shit," And when I replied, "I couldn't give a shit like you to a bitch like that," he hadn't been able to answer me, which was weird for him.

Later on when I asked him if he wanted another drink he just didn't answer me at all, which again wasn't exactly unlike Colin 'cause he wasn't one for stating the obvious, but I still thought it was kinda rude at the time.

This just wasn't Colin though. I really should say this now. It totally wasn't.

Usually it would've been, like the same but funnier: a shared joke rather than him just talking across me without noticing my reaction. Like he, I dunno, for example, if you ever asked Colin what time it was he'd say, "What the hell does it matter?" or something like this: but he'd always wait for you to like, laugh or give him some back or tell him to stop being a twat. It was just his sense of humour.

What I mean is... well Colin wasn't as much of a cunt as a lot of people thought he was. He'd kinda be sensitive to you and understand if one of his comments had gone too far. At least with me he would. But on this day he didn't really seem to care.

I don't actually wanna talk about this anymore 'cause for a lot of reasons I don't like discussing this particular meeting with Colin.

I met Colin in High Lanes, we had a conversation and it

was on the day when I woke up with the fizzing sound in my head for the first time. That's it. That's all that needs to be said.

ELEVEN

So when I came back with the drinks Colin had gone, which was no real surprise to me, and after I'd got through the first of the two pints and smoked a couple more fags I wasn't really that bothered.

So I sat there thinking about what the hell I was gonna do with my day.

Yeah, my dad used to drink at High Lanes. Not really got anything to do with me sitting there then and I don't think I even thought about this at the time. But he did; quite often actually. Although I'd been too young to ever join him.

Anyway, after a while I found myself listening to the barman and old guy going on at each other. They were the only other people in the pub still, standing and sitting in exactly the same place as they seemed to have been doing all day.

At the moment I started listening they were talking about the difference between arrogance and confidence, arguing over whether you could separate one from the other; where you could draw the line. (Although it was difficult to tell who was for each argument 'cause they were just sort of chewing over all the possible points of view without really agreeing or disagreeing on anything).

It was when I went to the bar for my fourth pint that I joined in. By then they'd moved on to discussing all the brews of beer they liked. They stopped talking as I approached the bar, both looking at me, just like most old men stare at you when you walk into a pub in Bracksea, and I said, "Yeah I really don't notice the difference myself."

Then as they both made eye contact with each other I said, "I guess you're pretty confident you know more about beer than I do?" and although the barman was kinda like, "Yeah, whatever mate," the old guy smiled saying, "You're a bit young to be drinking at this time of day aren't you?" And I said, "Well, it is the summer holidays," and they both like laughed a bit. Then the barman glanced at the old guy and sarcastically said, "It's all right for some," while the old man replied, "The joys of youth eh?"

After that the old guy told the barman to pour me a Firkintons and before I knew it I was at the bar with them, no longer paying for my drinks.

They asked how old I was and why I wasn't, "Out with some nice young lady today," and gave me a bit of hassle about my clothes but soon it was more like the same way as their conversations had been before, except this time I was included.

What we talked about I don't really wanna go into 'cause there's no point or anything. But it was cool to sit there talking to a couple of strangers for a bit. And they were pretty chilled out.

When the sixth pint was finished though I was feeling quite tired. I'd already been to the bogs about a million times (they seemed to find it funnier each time I went) and my head kept like dropping and it was getting hard to pay much attention to what we were saying so I felt it was time to go home.

It's all a bit of a blur as I imagine myself now walking out of the pub. I know I'd taken ages to get around to letting them know I was gonna go, sitting there like plucking up the courage to say I was leaving but that when I finally did take off it all happened well quickly. Like, I said, "I have to go," and next thing I was out the door.

When I got in my mum was back from work and there was some pie and chips waiting for me in the oven.

I grabbed the oven gloves, took the plate out, put it on a tray and got some coke out the fridge. It was quite cool, pissing around preparing my dinner. I remember my movements were well quick as I did all the things needed to sort the stuff. Like, get the tray, flick on the kettle, grab the oven gloves, take the plate out, put it on the tray, grab the tomato sauce off the shelf, decide I couldn't be arsed with tea so diving for the coke out of the fridge and grabbing a glass from the top cupboard, pouring the coke, putting the top back on and shoving it back in the fridge, kicking open the cutlery draw, grabbing a knife and fork, then grabbing the tray in one hand and the glass in the other.

My mum was in the front room on the sofa watching TV when I walked in and I sat down next to her.

As my arse hit the sofa I remember looking at her out of the corner of my eye, wondering whether she might be able to smell my breath and if it might've been a better idea to sit in the other chair. Then as watched her some more (like at intervals) I began wondering if it'd be a good idea to talk a bit first, or if it was okay to simply relax in front of the TV as I usually did – for some reason I really wanted to ask how her day had been.

I started to eat my dinner, saying, "Cheers mum," and looked at the programme she was watching (pig farmers moaning about how they were all going out of business; pretty boring) and after a bit said, "So, how was work?"

Before she answered I remember we heard a sudden crash of thunder from outside followed by the sound of heavy rain throwing itself against the windows. My mum said to me (or at least in my direction), "So this is supposed to be fucking summer then?" and then she got up, walking out to the kitchen with her plate, tray and empty glass in her hand.

TWELVE

I'd finished dinner, watched a bit of TV and was now on my bed listening to some Planquez with all the lights turned off. It was the first album: the good one. The one where they're basically ripping off The Pins but it doesn't matter 'cause it's well decent.

I was lying there feeling pretty relaxed but it was the last song (*Trees of England* – the heaviest and longest track). I knew as it got closer to finishing that it was time to make a decision as to what to do with my night. That is, whether to put on another CD or actually do something.

I felt like going out again. My mum was on the phone in her bedroom to someone and had been for ages. The TV was free but I'd been watching it all morning and couldn't be arsed with any more; at least in my own house.

When the CD finished everything was suddenly totally silent. There I was, lying there in the darkness, completely alone.

I remember saying (to myself), "Time for a plan," before rolling off the bed onto the carpet.

It was around eight o'clock and I guessed Duncan would probably be in; reckoning the idea of getting caned for the rest of the night seemed like the perfect way to finish off my day. So I put on my Patterson hoody, flares, whacked on my brown jacket ('cause it was still raining a bit, although not as much), put ten quid in my pocket just in case; and grabbed my walkman off the desk.

I shouted, "I'm going out!" to my mum as I passed her bedroom but there was no reply as I went down the stairs. I took my shoes and then I was out the door, into the night.

I made my way down the road in the rain, buttoning up my jacket and putting my hood up as I went towards the junction for the second time that day. (Yeah, I remember as I saw High Lanes coming into view I started wondering if Colin would be there again but decided it was unlikely).

I got to Duncan's five minutes later and banged on the door, hoping he wouldn't take too long to answer. The rain was at the stage where it's difficult to tell if it's gonna get worse or stop suddenly. But it wasn't the rain that was pissing me off. It was the wind, which had picked up a treat.

I'd been waiting for quite a while and had shouted through the letterbox a hell of a lot of times before I noticed the bit of paper stuck to the door.

It said:

COLIN AND I HAVE GONE TO LONDON
BACK NEXT WEEK

And then underneath, in smaller, more scribbled writing was written:

CHAMBERS WHERE THE FUCK ARE YOU!!!!????

I'LL BE AT THE TRAIN STATION.

The first thing I thought was like, "What the fuck?" But after a couple of minutes I remembered Duncan saying something about how he'd had, "The day off on Wednesday," and, "Did you fancy coming over?"

I couldn't remember anything about London though; nothing at all.

I stood there on the doorstep wondering what to do next and rolled a fag. My reckoning was the note had probably been written hours before but there was always the possibility Duncan had just left. So I was then left with the fact that I really didn't wanna go to London.

I mean, yeah, I could imagine Duncan saying, "Come on, it's London!" and in some ways he did have a point. But I couldn't help feeling there was no way in hell, like I felt really strongly that there was no way at all I was gonna wake up in London the next morning. So I had to make a decision: go to the train station and risk seeing Duncan or go home feeling like I'd done nothing with my night.

I looked at my watch: it said, *eight ten*. This gave me thirty minutes before the last train out of Bracksea.

I remember thinking, (and actually said out loud too), "If I see the last train leave, at least I can tell Duncan I tried."

*

On the walk down to the train station the weather was clearing up. It felt pretty cold though and the street was eerily silent (apart from the wind). I had my walkman with me but didn't turn it on. I figured I was gonna be a while at the train station and wanted to have something to look forward to once I'd got there. Also the station at Bracksea is a good place for joint butts and my plan was to find a couple of good ones, sit down on one of the benches, put on my walkman and spark up.

When I got to the station though there was fuck all there: not even anything worth trying; just in case. I considered going to the offie for a beer to make the wait a bit more enjoyable but then remembered it was a Wednesday and it'd be closed. So I sat there, wondering for a while how I was gonna pass the time but thinking at least I still had my walkman and sitting on a bench, smoking some fags and listening to a bit of music didn't seem so bad.

I put on the radio rather than tape, tuning in to John Bank who was playing some sort of half Hawaiian half gypsy type music which I'd never heard of before. It was pretty cool actually and made me feel more alive; less alone than I guess I really was.

Before long the train came in and I watched all the people getting off. It was a mixed crowd and I remember guessing where all of them had come from, why they were arriving in Bracksea at that time of night – some lads who looked like they'd been out in Firkinton, a couple of people in suits who were obviously returning from work (fuck that!) and a woman with a baby and I couldn't work out what her story was. She looked too distressed to be coming back from a friend's house or something.

I rolled another fag, taking my time and thought (and said), "If Duncan doesn't come before this train leaves then I don't have to go to London and all I need to do is roll this fag, smoke it and by the time I've finished the train will have gone and I'll have done my bit."

The program on the radio changed and they started playing this hardcore shit. The people disappeared and the guard closed all the doors; pacing up and down, with a cigarette too. He glanced at me a couple of times before looking up and down the carriages, clicked whatever it is they click and the train slowly moved off.

*

The music was growing on me and I felt pretty relaxed once the train had gone so I rolled another fag to celebrate.

I was just sparking up, going back through my mind who'd come off the train and whether it was worth having another scan for joint butts when I heard the sound of someone running: a sound which was getting closer. I looked over at the entrance, half scared half interested about who it was gonna be 'cause, actually weirdly I half expected it to be Colin.

Before long a figure kinda smashed through the gates and then, I dunno, sort of like landed on the edge of the platform.

It was Bog-Boy from Price-Savers: "Fucking Bog-Boy!" I remember thinking. "My prayers are answered."

Bog-Boy stood there looking up and down the platform, all confused and that. Then he walked towards me, quickly and all like with intent.

He didn't recognise me at first. He was like, "Excuse me mate do you know what time the last train comes?"

And I looked at him for a moment before answering, 'cause it was a bit confusing at first how he hadn't cottoned on as to who I was. But finally I turned down my walkman and simply said, "You've just missed it mate."

He realised who I was then; maybe it was my voice. He came out with, "You work in Price-Savers don't you?" which I didn't bother responding to 'cause he already knew the answer so there was no point. But then remembering I

46

had to play it cool I started off with a bit of sympathy and said, "That sucks man. So how are you gonna get home now?"

He was still looking confused though and asked me if I was sure the train had gone, like he didn't believe me or something.

I said, "Honestly it's gone," and, "I know, it's shit man, the last train's well early!" And 'cause he was still looking at me funny I slowly said, "Because it's Wednesday," and his face suddenly changed as he like, I dunno... grasped the situation?

I was like, "So what are you gonna do now?" with him replying that he didn't know, looking at my cigarette and at me, asking me what I was doing: and it was then I suddenly took in why he hadn't believed me before.

I thought for a moment about how to respond, then realising it was the perfect opportunity for my opening, told him I was looking for joint butts; which I knew being "Bog-Boy", he'd appreciate.

But when I asked, "You haven't got any gear have you?" he just looked at me with this sort of disgust on his face, saying, "Nah mate," and walked off.

THIRTEEN

The next time I was in Price-Savers, which was a Saturday, I was putting out strawberries by the front entrance when this girl walked up to me and asked, "Are you Chambers?" and when I replied, "Yeah," she said, "I've got a message for you."

She was well pretty actually. Not like stunning or anything but somehow this made her more attractive. Normal but still fit if you know what I mean. She had long red hair (like, *dyed* red), was just a bit shorter than me and was wearing a white tank top, jeans, and sandals – and I remember too that she smelt of chewing gum; mint flavour.

I looked at her, at her eyes, and didn't feel nervous for some reason (not that I'd usually feel this way about a girl but she *was* pretty fit). I said, "So what's the message?" and she looked down sort of shyly and was like, "Well, it's not really a message; just that your friend's outside." And then she said, like shyly again but this time pretty quickly, "Umm, some guy with long hair. He said to tell you he was outside."

As she spoke her hair sort of jumped about, around her face, which was quite cute. And I also remember noticing straight away how she had a nice voice too. Kinda sweet but not too girly if you know what I mean and I've always liked that in a girl; a nice voice that is.

I said, "Cool," then, "Cheers," and... well, she just sort of walked away without saying anything else, but displaying, yeah, a pretty sweet arse: tight but not too small; just right.

*

When I got outside I looked all over for Duncan before finally finding him round the corner waiting for me in the disabled trolleys bit. He was kinda standing there doing nothing. No fag or joint in his hand or anything. Just standing there, staring into space.

I got up to him and he jumped in surprise at seeing me, like totally out of his skin, and then said, really slowly, "Hey man, where the hell were you last Wednesday?" obviously stoned already and that.

I scanned the forecourt to see if there were any managers around, like walking to or from the petrol station or something, but there weren't – only customers: mostly families with their trolleys and their shopping and their big cars with big boots, loading up their shit for the week, trying to make their kids shut up and not giving a fuck about me being outside when I should've be working. (It was the pensioners that you had to watch out for. They were the ones who had nothing better to do than complain about you to your manager).

So yeah, there was no one worth worrying about so I blagged a cigarette off Duncan and sparked up.

I looked around again and then back at Duncan who was saying, "Hey man, you all right?" and I said, "Yeah," before apologising for forgetting he'd had the day off on Wednesday. I said about going to the station to meet him as soon as I'd seen the note and that, and apparently he'd left in the morning anyway; although the weird thing was, he didn't remember writing a note: actually when he told me this I didn't find it strange at the time, I just called him a, "Fuckin' stoner," and asked if he was stoned already with him laughing and saying, "Yeah," and we laughed (or at least talked humorously) about: what better thing was there to do on a Saturday morning?

Anyway, Duncan said he was, "Just passing by," but had come to tell me about a beach party that was going on in Bracksea which apparently everyone was going to, and for me to tell Bradby, Neale and, "Anyone else," about it too.

I said, "Cool," and, "Of course," and he said, "Cool," and that I could meet him at his or just meet him at the beach. I said I'd meet him at the beach.

Yeah, thinking about it now the reason Duncan didn't come in to Price-Savers was probably 'cause he used to have a job there. You know, how he didn't wanna go back to his old place of work and all; although I didn't consider this at the time.

But actually it was quite nice standing out in the sun talking to Duncan when I was supposed to be working. I remember wishing I didn't have to go back in and that it would've been so cool to walk off with Duncan to wherever the hell he was going next, spark up a joint and like soak up the sunny day.

*

I walked back in and carried on with strawberries. Already the display was looking like shit again. Totally stripped (yeah it was a buy-one-get-one-free-thing). I put out the rest of the strawberries from my L-shape, which was only a couple of cases, and went out the back for more.

Bradby was unloading boards in the warehouse when I got in there. I started telling him I'd just seen Duncan and about the beach party but yeah, I was only as far as, "Hey, Duncan was here just now," when he cut me short, asking, "Are the strawberries filled up yet?"

I looked at him, kinda disbelievingly I guess ('cause obviously seeing Duncan was far more important than fucking strawberries), but then thought, "Whatever," and just said how it was, "Fucking impossible," to keep the display looking good, describing how the customers were, "Like vultures," hoping he'd laugh at least.

But he didn't laugh and still looking serious asked how many cases of strawberries we had left. When I said, "I'm just going in for some more now," he was like, "We've got shit loads of golden delicious," and, "See if you can get some of them on the front table too."

I went in the chiller, cursing Bradby under my breath, grabbed the rest of the strawberries, threw them on my L-shape, took three cases of golden delicious off a stack that was towered up almost touching the roof of the chiller and pushed my L-shape out again.

As I passed Bradby he said, "Sorry mate, bit of a tough morning today," and I turned around to see him standing there with his shirt hanging out, hair all messed up, sweating and that, looking kinda, I dunno, like almost... pathetic I guess.

And I really wanted to tell him what a twat he looked, or at least was starting to become. But all I could say was, "Yeah, don't worry about it," and he smiled and I smiled too (which was a fake smile) with him then turning around, carrying on with the board he was working on: all like satisfied he'd made me feel better or something.

So anyway, I was out on the shop floor for ages next 'cause The Terminator had found me putting the golden delicious out and said for me to make it into a proper display, find a new place for the strawberries on the side counter, and after that Hitler had found me, asked why produce was in, "Such a state," and told me to, "Do a dress down and quality check."

Then as I was doing this The Terminator came back and, after asking why I hadn't finished the golden delicious display, told me I was, "On second lunch," and how there were four L-shapes loaded up in the chiller, "Ready to go out now," and how I was to keep produce running until everyone got back.

So there I was, working on the department by myself for an hour, putting up with all the customer queries and complaints about, "Are there any more...?" and, "Do you have any...?" and, "Why aren't there any...?" and, "Where's your manager?" while trying to put out the four L-shapes (I only managed two) and keep it all looking nice. Kinda stressful to say the least; but I didn't really care.

Second lunch was shit as usual (no one goes second lunch). I ended up having to sit with the trolley guy who was telling me all about how the government were trying to turn Skipton into a nuclear waste dump; how he'd seen a programme about it on TV the night before.

Because of seeing Duncan in the morning I guess, and also 'cause of the trolley guy doing my head in, I went for a fag outside rather than in the smoking room.

It was still hot out, although there was a slight breeze which made it pretty comfortable.

51

I remember thinking as I stood there smoking my cigarette about how much a whole day of my life was really worth. Like how the only reason I wasn't out in the sun was 'cause of the forty quid I was earning on my shift. And how it was impossible to put a price on a day of someone's life and what the hell was I doing there putting out fucking fruit and vegetables when I could be out in the sun with Duncan?

After my fag though I looked at my watch to see it was two-fifty which meant I only had two hours left, was still owed a tea break, so it could've been worse. I mean, at least I still had a beach party to go to later.

*

Neale was on our department again when I got back on produce (he'd been with the freezer crew all morning). I told him about the beach party, he said, "Cool," and how it was, "About time," someone had organised something like that, what with the weather and all.

The Terminator had a right go at me about what a mess the department had been in when he'd got back from lunch and was being sarcastic saying, "You must've worked really hard."

Yeah there were like five members of staff working on produce at that point; even Vader was there with his jacket off helping to put stuff out. The Terminator was like, "This is what the department *should* look like." Totally all proud as if it was him who'd done all the work. And then not long after he said he was, "Going to the office to do some paperwork," and, "Do you think you can manage this time?"

So before long it was just me and Neale on produce; yeah, Bradby went to the office with The Terminator while the other people who were helping went back to their departments.

The section was looking well good. Me and Neale talked about how, "Obviously it is," 'cause of course The Terminator had got like the whole shop to help him. After a while of walking around chatting and not doing a hell of a lot

– there wasn't really a hell of a lot to do, it was afternoon; there weren't that many customers any more – I persuaded Neale to go for a tea break with me.

At first he was like, "We'd better not," and, "You saw what kind of mood The Terminator's in," but all in all he didn't take so much persuasion. He knew damn well if we got caught I was the one who'd get the blame anyway.

We had a drink (he had tea, I had coffee) and shared this apple tart thing which was really nice. We talked about Price-Savers, Bradby, how there was no way in hell we were gonna end up getting, "Stuck in this shit-hole," and then talked for a bit about what we were gonna do once the summer was over. Neale told me he'd finally decided on studying *Business and Computing* at Shingham University. I had no idea what I was gonna do and he was telling me I should go to uni. Actually he even said I should go to Shingham uni with him (and that it was easy to get in to) 'cause it was, "Better than getting a job," and was supposed to be a well good laugh. But I still wasn't sure if I could be bothered with having to study shit for any longer; or maybe even ever; like, for the rest of my life; which is what I said.

Our tea break lasted ages but we didn't get caught. When we got back out there was no one on the department and it was looking a bit messy so we loaded up a couple of L-shapes, put them out together and after tidying up a bit it was time to go home.

Neale's girlfriend met him outside, looking totally fit, wearing one of those short summer dresses, which was blowing about around her legs.

She said, "Hi" to me, I said, "Hi," then said, "See you tonight," to Neale with him saying, "Cool," and then they walked off. As I watched them continue in the direction of Neale's house (which is right opposite Price-Savers) I remember thinking, *fucking bastard*.

So anyway, I stood there rolling a fag watching Neale and his girlfriend walking towards his house, thinking what a bastard Neale was and wondering what I could do with the rest of my day, like, before the beach party. It was hot and nice and I didn't feel like going home yet, the memory of seeing Duncan disappear into the sun that morning still being fresh in my mind.

It was then, as I was standing there and had just lit my cigarette, when I suddenly got the idea I could go to Duncan's dealer's house to score some gear. I'd only ever been there once and had only stood outside waiting for Duncan; I didn't actually know his dealer at all but remember thinking, "Fuck it," and, "So what if I don't know him," and that going there and giving it a try seemed like an adventure.

I drew on my cigarette, watching the trolley guy sweating it out in the heat and shouted, "Fucking Price-Savers man!"

I then put on my walkman, which had a mix-tape in and *Killer Flowers* (an old Mary Hefner song) came on.

Drawing on my cigarette again, with Mary singing about *those colours that make me wanna cry*, I began my trek to the other side of Skipton.

FOURTEEN

When I got to the house, *It's What You Wanna Be (Cut the Crap)* by Nictane was playing in my ears which is a well heavy song. I was kinda slightly singing to it and remember realising, like as I knocked on the door, that it'd probably be a good idea to shut up.

I turned off my walkman with everything going quiet, abruptly, and actually, hate to admit it but I felt a little bit scared all of a sudden. Like, what the hell was I doing there standing outside this drug dealer's house?

The door opened and Duncan's dealer was standing there with a drying up cloth in his hand looking at me as if to say, "Who the fuck are you?"

While there was me standing there looking back at him wondering what the hell I was supposed to do.

I was like, "Umm," and, "Hey are you..." but then realising I'd forgotten his name (and actually wasn't sure if I'd ever known his name in the first place: Duncan had always referred to him as, "I've gotta go and see my dealer,") I figured asking him if he was who I knew damn well he was, was a stupid question anyway, so I just said, "Hey, I'm a friend of Duncan's."

He stared at me, like interrogatively a bit, before saying, "Who the fuck is Duncan?" and I remember it was hard to tell if he was joking or angry or whatever.

I said, "He buys stuff off you sometimes... long hair, about twenty, comes from Bracksea?" And he replied, "Look mate I don't know what you're talking about," and then just kinda stood there as if he was waiting for me to say something else. Actually it seemed like he was about to close the door on me, so I said, "I know Alex and Paul too," (dunno why; this just sort of came out).

I waited for a response for what seemed like ages before Duncan's dealer suddenly started laughing and was like, "*Alex and Paul?*" sort of sarcastically, saying, "*Bloody hell!*"

I remember I could hear the sound of a TV in the background playing a cartoon or something and there was the also the noise of a baby which was, I dunno, a sort of gurgling sound; it wasn't crying or anything but I could still tell it was a baby.

Duncan's dealer shouted back into the house, sarcastically again, saying, "Some guy says he knows Alex and Paul and wants to buy something from me."

A woman then came to the door. She had tattoos and piercings – bit of a shit description I know, but that's pretty much all I remember about her; apart from that she also had long black hair, which was wet – and was holding a baby that was sucking on a dummy.

The woman said, "Oh for God's sake Tim, stop teasing him," and, "He's just a kid."

Then Tim (assuming that was his name now; it was either Tim or Tom) looked back at me, smiled and raised his eyes saying, "Okay, I guess you'd better come in."

*

So Tim was all right actually. When I got in he even offered to make me a cup of tea – well, he said tea was in the pot, he didn't actually offer to make me one.

The lady disappeared upstairs and I remember wondering whether to follow Tim into the kitchen or to wait in the corridor so I kinda like, hovered.

Yeah, the house was smaller than I'd expected; at least it'd looked bigger from the outside. And the downstairs was just this tiny corridor, a kitchen and a front room, which was also pretty small. There was a little girl in the front room watching TV and as I waited for Tim I stood under the doorframe looking at the screen. Some cartoon with robots beating each other up. As I watched this like, head robot who was obviously a bad guy was beating up this female white robot, who was quite fit as far as robots go, and the bad robot was laughing while the female robot was saying, "Please!" and, "No!"

Tim came back with the tea saying, "So what is it you're after?" and when I told him I just wanted a bit of block he

56

said, "What?" and I said, "Resin," and he was like, "Oh, right," and, "How much?" and I was like, "About ten quid's worth."

He then said, "I'll tell you what," or something like this ('cause I didn't hear him clearly), and went out to the kitchen again where I could hear him rummaging around while meantime there was this team of four robots (a blue one, a red one, a green one and a yellow one) racing through this futuristic metropolis type city obviously on their way to rescue the girl.

The polythene bag that Tim brought back was huge. It was full of weed, like proper weed. Tim held the bag up, saying, "This stuff's the business." (Yeah he didn't seem to care about his daughter – or whoever the girl was – being there which I thought was, I dunno, a bit weird actually).

I asked, "How much?" and Tim replied, "Thirty five," which he said was a very good price considering, "the quality of the stuff," and I wasn't sure if he was ripping me off or not but there wasn't really a hell of a lot I could say or do; I mean the bag was pretty big. So I said, "Okay, cool."

Tim then said, "I'll tell you what, I'll let you try some first," and opening the bag, taking a huge clump of weed out he proceeded to roll a joint.

The girl just sat there, still watching cartoons, totally un-phased.

As Tim rolled up I asked him, "How's business?" with him replying that it was, "Always good in the summer," and when I said about how much better it was smoking joints in the sun he laughed, answering, "That must be the reason."

Then he laughed again when I said that it, "Must be good to not have a job," looking at me kinda funny, saying, "In my dreams mate," which I figured meant he must've had another job on the side or something.

Anyway, it's all a bit of a blur after this. I remember the robots rescued the girl, but there again I also remember them killing the bad robot (like, totally killing him) and I'm not sure if this would've really happened in a kids cartoon.

I also remember... yeah, I thought I'd got a free joint out

of Tim but the way it ended up he got a free joint out of me.

But still, I didn't really care at the time. It was quite fun sitting there and I felt happy I'd taken the opportunity to do something interesting with my afternoon.

FIFTEEN

Pretty soon I was feeling a bit sick. There'd been no tobacco in the joint at all; also the front room was tiny and by then full of smoke. I had to get out so saying, "Bye," to Tim and the girl (who said her name was Jessica) I bundled myself out of the door.

Everything was well bright when I got outside. It was like, blinding. I was finding it hard to focus on anything. I remember the street as just shapes of houses but sort of abstract shapes, like an abstract picture: a roof here, a wall there, a hedge there; all a bit of a mess. Then, as I turned on my walkman Nictane suddenly blasted into my ears, scaring the shit out of me, and I said, "Fucking hell!" like really loud. I remember ripping the earphones from my ears, reaching for the volume button, fumbling around for it, and my heart was then beating really fast.

I stumbled up the road, rolling a cigarette as I went. As I drew on it my mouth felt dry and tasted dry and weird but it was kinda comforting too.

I got to the top, went through the alleyway and then was at the bus stop. Once there I looked at the bus times for the next one to Bracksea which was a thirty minute wait so… actually not the sort of thing I usually would've done but, yeah at the time for some reason the fact I'd obviously just missed the bus really pissed me off (like: *really*) and I shouted, "FUCKING BOLLOCKS!" hitting the timetable with the whole bus shelter rattling.

I looked around, wondering what to do, like whether to wait or not. Then I thought (and said), "Fuck it," and started walking.

So yeah, anyway, I'd been walking for ages when I found myself heading towards the beach, and it was like as this realisation hit me I decided to go back to Bracksea that way. My walkman was playing, the sun was shining, I had my tobacco; the bag of weed in my pocket. It was a good excuse for a walk I felt.

I was a bit hungry though so I stopped off at a garage first to get some crisps, a chocolate bar and a pastie (Hoola-Hoops, an Aero, and Ginsters chicken and mushroom). I remember taking ages with my money and the guy behind the counter being really patient. As I left I said, "Cheers for being nice to me," or something like this; then was wishing I'd simply kept my mouth shut, although actually what I'd said wasn't so bad and at least I'd been polite in showing my appreciation for good service.

So the beach at Skipton is a bit of a shit-hole but you can walk to Bracksea along the shore with it getting better as you go (kinda less gravely, more beach-like). I used to do that walk quite often with my parents when I was a kid actually; but then it was easier to do, and actually that's not important: although the fact of this route being familiar to me is probably the reason why I'd found myself subconsciously heading down there in the first place.

The houses dwindled away, fishing boats appeared, I cut across the train line and then the sea was right in front of me.

I could see Bracksea in the distance along the shore. It wasn't dark yet – the last time I'd seen this view it'd been the, "Lights of Bracksea," town (as my dad used to say) but this time... well, what stood out most was the Bracksea school buildings, with the golf course behind and the cliffs further on.

Once at the beach I stopped and stood there looking at the view, thinking about Bracksea and how small it was; how there was a big world out there but I'd spent most of my life on that tiny patch of land... and yeah, I then started getting this idea of how cool it'd be to fly there: like, out to sea, over to Bracksea: to be able to float around like a seagull, letting the breeze carry me wherever I wanted to go, not to have to worry about money or getting a job or finding some fucking purpose to life. Just float about doing whatever.

I lit up a fresh cigarette and started along the gravely path.

SIXTEEN

I'd been walking for a while and was just over half way to Bracksea when I stopped for a rest. My walkman batteries were running low so I turned it off, sitting there listening to the sound of the sea; the waves, lapping onto the shore continuously and that.

It was dusk by then. I could see the sun and the moon at the same time. Both were big, while the sky had an orange glow to it.

I took out my papers and stuck three together, then the bag of weed and took a small clump, carefully arranging it into a line along the papers. I took out my backy, covered the green stuff with brown, picked it all up and rolled it around between my fingers; ripped off a roach from my rizla packet, rolled it all together, licked it and finally held the new joint in my hand, admiring my creation.

As I sparked up and breathed it all in I remember appreciating how I was having was one of those perfect moments: the dusk, the sound of the waves, being alone sitting there, at one with my thoughts.

Yeah, my thoughts: again a bit of a blur as I recollect but I know for certain I thought about Neale's girlfriend in that dress, imagining how good it would've been to lift it up and like run my hand along her arse.

I also thought about the Price-Saver's girl that morning, but although this started off as a similar fantasy, somehow I never managed to be able to totally concentrate on her in a, I dunno, in any sort of sexual way or whatever.

Anyway, I followed the same routine with skinning up and marvelling at what a cool moment I was having three times (like three joints finished) before Colin turned up.

By then it was nearly dark and stars were starting to appear in the sky. The sun had gone but the moon was really bright so I could still see everything pretty clearly.

I was looking over in the direction of Bracksea, watching the lights turn on one by one and could hear the sound of crunching, with there being a slight fizzing noise that had started too which I thought nothing of at the time. I wasn't really paying attention to anything though, other than to like catch or notice each light as it appeared. But then out of nowhere I caught a glimpse of movement to my right and when I turned to look I could see a figure approaching and it was Colin.

He still had his head shaved and, yeah he was wearing the same clothes as he'd been wearing in High Lanes. He had more colour to his face this time though. Maybe it was the sea air; who knows?

So anyway, as he walked up to me he said, "Hey Chambers, how're you doing?" and I wondered for a moment what exactly he meant by this so I said, "What do you mean?"

SEVENTEEN

I liked this meeting with Colin. This particular encounter was well fun. We talked about my day; I told him all about what it'd been like at work. I said about going to Duncan's dealer's house (and Colin reckoned I'd been ripped off) and I even mentioned the fit girl at Price-Savers who'd told me about Duncan being outside and how I'd felt a connection with her.

We talked about Bradby as well with Colin telling me not to worry about him too much and also to, "Give the guy a break," which I thought was probably right; although there was no way for Colin to properly understand exactly what it felt like being ordered around by your mate. Actually I then started thinking how Bradby would've never talked to Colin like that but I didn't say anything.

I also told Colin about Neale's girlfriend, him replying how he wished he'd had the chance to see her and agreeing with me about how Neale was a, "Lucky bastard."

Yeah, originally it'd been a bit tense after Colin had asked me how I was doing and I'd thought he was having a go. But he'd apologised and then said that he was sorry for being, "A bit of a shit," the other day and said about how being dead was, "A bit of a drag."

So yeah, this meeting was pretty nice. It was like, exactly what I'd been wanting to do: get stoned with Colin. I missed that. He was obviously in a better mood and... he put me in a better mood too.

Even so, although it was good I felt like, yeah, it wasn't real and I knew it wasn't real this time, even though it felt real, and... well, I dunno. But anyway, I think Colin must've picked up on it too 'cause at the end (like, just before he went) he said, "You know, I may not be around for a while after this," and when I asked him, "Why?" he said, "I just don't think it's a good idea."

At first I didn't say much to this, just something like, "Fair enough," or, "A man's gotta do what a man's gotta do," or some dumb joke but later when he got up to leave I asked when the next time I'd see him would be and he said, "I don't know." Suddenly it hit me like how, I dunno, like how the happiest I'd been that day was at and around the moment Colin had appeared. But when I told him this he simply replied that it wasn't true and how it was time that I started to realise this, or something.

I really wanted to stop him from going, to make him promise to come back soon, or even to grab his legs and say, "Come with me to the beach party at least," but I didn't. When he got up to leave I merely said, "See you later," and he said, "Yeah man," and as he walked away back in the direction he'd come from I turned my head to once again look at the lights of Bracksea.

*

What happened next is a bit weird. And to be honest I'm not one hundred percent sure if it happened at all actually, but yeah, I'm gonna tell it as though it did.

Basically, what went on was… well, I'd had the first joint with Tim, then three by myself and two with Colin; and although the joints I was rolling weren't that strong I was still feeling a bit strange. Like, how before Colin had appeared I guess I was pretty wasted but once he'd gone the feeling was more; well: *fucked* actually.

So what I did was I rolled a fag and got up and started walking around. And yeah this was all right at first, but after a while I started to feel a bit messy. I wasn't walking in a straight line and also I'd turned my walkman on again and the music (I can't remember what exactly) was sounding like really quick, random and all over the place.

Pretty soon I'd stopped and was lying down but when I closed my eyes my head was spinning, really fast around and around. Like when you used to go on a roundabout when you were a kid going round and round for ages before jumping off and afterwards when you were laying there everything would still be moving. That's what I felt like.

I sat up wondering what I could do to make myself feel

better. Then I decided to roll another joint.

So there I was going through the same routine, same amount of green stuff, same amount of brown, my rizla packet falling apart.

I took in the first drag which made me feel a little calmer. The second drag was even better. The third kinda made me feel a bit sick but was still good. The fourth…

Well anyway, it was around this point (at least the joint was still in my hand) when I noticed the fire on the beach in the distance. Not a big fire or anything. Like a campfire I suppose, if you know what I mean. And there was also the noise of music, a faint noise, and as I looked over to Bracksea I could make out the silhouettes of people around the fire with the muffled sound of voices and I remembered about the beach party, realising that of course this was what it was.

So, as I said before, I'm not totally sure if this happened or not but as far as I'm concerned (at least as far as my memory goes) it did.

I was lying on the beach and I knew the party had started. I really wanted to go but at the same time I kinda didn't. It was like, in some ways I was happy with the idea of being at the party already but I sort of didn't wanna walk up there by myself and think about who to go up to first, what to say, and also to answer questions of what I was doing coming along the beach from the direction of Skipton, what had I been doing with my day and why?

I'm not sure though, maybe it was more than this. In some ways I didn't even like the idea of being at the party at all. Like, what was the point?

Although at the same time I was in the mood for the party and it was probably the best place to be considering how wasted I was. But I dunno. Maybe it was seeing Colin. Maybe for some reason I was feeling pretty aware for the first time in a while how alone I'd been feeling and the idea of suddenly not being alone and there in the middle of all those people, half of them who I probably wouldn't even know, seemed like… maybe I was feeling alone and that was just about okay but the possibility of feeling alone when I was surrounded by lots of people would've been worse.

But I still sort of wanted to go to the party.

I sat there wondering what to do, thought about rolling another joint but then made a cigarette instead. Then, and this is the weird part which is difficult to properly recollect... so I'm just gonna say what I must've done is that I must've finished my cigarette, stood up, taken all my clothes off, walked down to the sea and waded in.

I have this clear recollection of it being really fucking cold at first but getting used to it gradually, but of course there's always the chance this could be a distorted memory 'cause the sea is always like that when you go in. I definitely remember though (at least there's an image in my mind) that when I first started swimming out it was an amazing feeling; like freedom, being free. And I remember swimming on my back for ages and looking up at the moon, the stars which were all totally clear and bright, and it was an awesome view.

So yeah, I swam, or at any rate I have this memory of swimming, out to see and then over in the direction of the beach party.

The next thing which is really distinct in my mind is being opposite the party, still in the water, still naked but far enough out so no one knew I was there, trying to make out who was who. I could hear Graz's voice, and Sereme's. Charlotte was laughing and some people were shouting but I didn't know who they were. As I watched for longer I could make out Duncan's silhouette sitting with some other people around the fire while the rest of the bodies were sort of scattered around and I could see that some of them were drinking out of wine bottles, some from cans; or at least the movements of their hands were giving off this impression.

And music was playing and everyone was happy, with the lights of Bracksea behind them and the white cliffs reflecting the moon further on.

So yeah, this is how I first saw the beach party. It looked like fun. But the more I watched, the harder it was to imagine myself being a part of it.

EIGHTEEN

I woke up on the beach. It was dark, like black. I rolled over and looked at my watch. It said, one o'clock. I could hear the sound of wind and of the sea. To my left four robots were standing there, like towering over me.

In my memory I can still see them now if I close my eyes and remember. The same robots as the ones in the cartoon the girl Jessica had been watching: except seeing them in real life, they were a lot more, authentic I guess. All really big, about eight or nine foot tall and all very much... *built*: obviously really strong and that, with their big square robot muscles.

As in the cartoon there was a red one, a blue one, a green one and a yellow one. But the colours, they weren't totally covered in colour 'cause there were silver parts too around their joints, and their eyes were all the same: black, big but slanted, kinda oval shaped, stuck on their heads diagonally sort of thing.

The red one said, in a booming robot voice, "We need your help," and then, "You're coming with us," and I sort of said, "Okay," and got up.

Although I said, "Okay," the feeling of speaking was like, I could hear my words but it didn't feel as if I was making myself say them. It was just stuff coming out of my mouth.

I got to my feet, not especially scared for some reason; actually quite calm. The robots turned around in synchronisation and started walking into the blackness while I was trundling along behind them, not really feeling the need to argue: they weren't using the path and I had no idea as to where they were taking me.

As I think back now I can almost feel myself stumbling over the terrain of gravely, rocky ground, looking out for the odd gorse bush or rock to step over or around. And I can even feel the sweat running down my face as I struggle to keep up.

Anyway, it wasn't too long before I noticed the girl from Price-Savers was walking along next to me, her red hair flowing behind her in the wind (yeah, it was almost like cartoon hair or something).

I turned to look at her face and I remember that I wanted and tried to meet her eyes but she was just staring right ahead. So I started to think of something to say to her, maybe ask what the fuck was going on, how she'd got there and where we were being taken when I suddenly realised she was naked, like completely.

Then I looked down at my own body to see I was naked too.

*

I woke up on the beach. It was dark, like black. I rolled over and looked at my watch. It said, one o'clock. I could hear the sound of wind and of the sea.

I lay there for a bit, looking around for the four robots I'd just been dreaming about (although at this moment I wasn't totally sure what the hell was going on) but they were nowhere to be seen so I rolled over, found my tobacco and began making a fag, wondering why the hell I'd been looking around for four robots in the first place; then remembering the dream.

I got to my feet and sparked up. Everything was really black: except for the end of my cigarette, glowing in the darkness.

I stood there trying to put my head together, attempting to make sense of images of a man called Tim passing me a joint; a girl with red hair telling me to go outside; an image of Skipton as a nuclear waste dump; a small girl called Jessica quietly watching TV; the sound of Charlotte laughing; a fat Indian man smiling at me while handing me my receipt; a far away view of people drinking out of wine bottles and beer cans on a beach; four robots telling me to follow them 'cause they needed my help; Duncan asking if I was okay…

I looked around me, at the sea, the moon, then remembered the beach party and the fire and turned my gaze towards

69

Bracksea beach but I couldn't see hardly anything. Even Bracksea itself was almost invisible.

I said, "Everyone's sleeping," to myself, and laughed a bit before looking at my watch again to see it was still one o'clock and said (again to myself), "Time for bed," and started properly laughing; really loud and that.

My shoes were off for some reason. They were lying on the floor next to me and I put them on, singing this Pearls song to myself, *It's Up To You When You Want*; the one which Graz had once before described as the, "Perfect summer anthem," or something.

The chorus is:

We'll have a Southward-facing garden
That's what you want for me
They'll see a Southward-facing garden
Five times the man I used to be

I want a Southward-facing garden
It's what you want for me
They'll see a Southward-facing garden
We'll have your friends around for tea

(Pretty shit I know, but that's The Pearls for you.)

So I was singing this as I put on my shoes, getting to my feet and starting to kinda labour along the beach path still singing, still feeling pretty messy, still on my mission to get to Bracksea while there was still the chance of finding a beach party to go to.

NINETEEN

The first people I met while on my way along the beach were Ambra, Sereme, and this other guy who I knew to be Ambra's boyfriend – I'd never met the guy before but immediately knew who he was from his description: tall with a beard who looked about thirty but wasn't. From his appearance he at least seemed too old to be going out with Ambra, who's my age: around eighteen at the time.

Ambra and Sereme were walking along arm in arm, clearly deep in conversation while the guy who was obviously Ambra's boyfriend was sort of moping around them, trailing behind a bit, throwing stones in the sea.

When Sereme saw me she was like, "Hey Chambers!" and ran up to give me a hug. Then she immediately gave me this sad face and said, "Where have you been Chambers?" in a childish sort of voice, which she sometimes used, before then saying, "We've missed you," which immediately got my back up actually 'cause I wasn't exactly sure who the "*We*" was supposed to be, but I let it go.

I said, "Well I'm here now," and she laughed, then sort of gave me a kiss, like, on the lips, almost a snog actually for some reason.

She was wearing a dark, sort of brown coloured (it was hard to tell) dress, her hair was up and she was wearing shit loads of make-up which looked… yeah it looked kinda weird under the moonlight. Really sort of bright but shadowy, like white and red colours but shaded around her face kinda perfectly. Her eyes though were smudged slightly, making it appear as if she might've been crying.

I said, "So how was the beach party?" and she turned back at Ambra with them sort of exchanging this glance and then Ambra said, "Don't ask," which made me think something had probably happened between Sereme and Graz – I remember thinking *Graz really is a git*; but not in a bad way; actually it almost made me smile, which I immediately felt guilty about.

I said, "You okay?" but before she'd got the chance to

answer Ambra's boyfriend came up to me with an introduction of, "All right mate, I'm Richard," saying, "So you're Chambers?" and, yeah, he was then looking at Ambra as if he was asking for some sort of confirmation or something, which I didn't understand 'cause Sereme had just a moment before shouted, "Hey Chambers," but Ambra was already talking to Sereme again in like a hushed tone (I couldn't make out what they were saying).

I said to Richard, "Have you guys just been to the beach party?" and he was like, "Well, we are on the beach," which I didn't understand at first but then realised it was some kinda joke and actually by this time he'd already said, "Yeah," and, "Are you going there now?" so I said, "No I'm just walking along the beach 'cause I fancied a walk in the dark just for fun," and that I wanted to look at the moon and the stars and the lights of Bracksea with the cliffs reflecting in the moonlight and it was now his turn to pause before he laughed uncertainly, replying, "Cool."

So I talked to Richard for a while, who was a bit posh but all right, and threw stones in the sea. Listening to him go on about how he loved Bracksea, how he wanted to live there, bring his kids up there 'cause of it being the, "Perfect place to spend your life," saying about the beach, the countryside all around, how Firkinton was only an hour's drive away and all.

Yeah, I wasn't sure what to say to all this really. I didn't wanna disagree 'cause he seemed so like passionate with what he was saying. And actually he was making a good point but I did say how, "It's different when you've been here all your life," to which he replied, "Maybe," and that he'd spent most of his life in Giglinham, which was, "A dump." I remember thinking then about how at least he'd had a decent football team to watch; when I said this he replied, "Yeah, that's true," and we talked about football for a bit.

After a while I asked him what the beach party was like, if it was still going on and he said, "Yeah, there're people still down there," so I said, "Cool," and, "I'm gonna head over there now I reckon."

Sereme and Ambra had walked a bit further up the beach by then, which I thought was kinda rude (like, not to me: to Richard), and actually I felt a bit sorry for him suddenly, having to follow his girlfriend around. When I asked, "So how come you guys aren't still there?" he was looking over at Ambra and all, "Yeah, well, you know…" but when I was like, "Do you fancy a quick joint?" he said, "No, it's okay," and that he didn't smoke.

So anyway, I said, "Bye," to Richard, shouted, "Bye," to Ambra and Sereme who both waved and then I carried on going along the beach.

It was about ten, fifteen minutes later before I started to hear voices. I saw the glow of a joint butt and pretty soon I could make out Duncan's long hair, then started to recognise Neale's voice and as I got closer I saw that Graz was the one smoking the joint.

It was Duncan, Neale, Graz, and two other guys who I recognised as mates of Graz's.

Neale was the first to say something as I approached, coming out with, "Shit, it's Chambers!" with everyone turning around to look.

Duncan was all like, "Man, I didn't think you were coming," and Neale was, "What the fuck happened to you?" asking where I'd been and that. And I wasn't sure what to say at first actually, like whether to tell them about my night, how much detail to go into ('cause I couldn't really be arsed to go into any of it, I just wanted to sit down), but then as I looked at them all sitting there I suddenly started wondering what was going on, like where was the party? So I simply made a joke about how I thought the party, "Would just be getting going around now," and laughed, asking, "What's happened to everyone?"

No one seemed to be interested in answering this question though, at least at first. Neale was just looking at me saying, "I tried to call you," sounding, worried or something. So finally I told them about going to score the gear off Tim saying this was where I'd been.

Duncan was like, "What?" and, "How much?" and when I told him he said, "You should've gone with me," and like how Tim was well dodgy and that; although when I showed them the bag of weed everyone (especially Graz's mates) was saying, "Wow," and, "Cool!" which made me feel a bit better.

I asked Graz what'd happened with Sereme as I sat down, accepting the joint from his mate as I did so, and lay back on the cobblestones (not sand unfortunately), satisfied how finally I'd made it to my destination, like how *now I can just relax and have a talk with Graz.*

But no, it wasn't to be 'cause everyone heard me when I said this and it was like, "What?" and, "How did you know?" and stuff so I had to tell them all about meeting Sereme and Ambra on the beach, why I'd come from that direction in the first place and how I'd walked all the way from Skipton – but I didn't go into too much detail; and was careful to leave out the part about Sereme kissing me (and of course the thing with Colin but this goes without saying).

No one said much to my story though, which was a bit of a surprise. Actually I remember it was only Graz who responded, asking me what Sereme had said.

I told him she hadn't said anything but that she'd just seemed sad. Then one of Graz's mates said, "So how come you knew it was 'cause of Graz?" and I remember I started to feel a bit awkward but luckily Duncan rescued me with a, "You look like you're wasted man," and everyone laughed.

I then said about Tim's joint putting me in such a state and it being the reason for me thinking it'd be a good idea to walk home from Skipton, how I'd gotten even more wasted along the way, which they thought was well funny.

So anyway, after this they were all telling me how the police had come to break up the party and, yeah, how Bradby had got arrested for basically nothing (he'd taken the piss out of a police officer, calling him a, "Dozy twat," but that was it) and had been taken away in a police car – at first I was like, "No way!" and actually thought they might've been winding me up but apparently it was true.

When I then asked how come they were all still there they said like how they'd decided to stay down the beach anyway, slagging everyone else off for being "Lame," and going home.

They did admit though that for the past hour they'd been taking turns to, "Go look-out," and then everyone, even me (although of course I hadn't been there at the time) was cracking up about this for ages. Yeah, for the rest of the night we kept making jokes saying, "I reckon you should go look-out," to each other; most of the time to Neale who was like, "Okay guys it's not funny any more," but the more we said it to him the funnier it was.

So this was basically how the night sort of ended for me: sitting on the beach with everyone and it actually being quite a good laugh. I thought a couple of times about Colin, how I reckoned he would've enjoyed sitting with us, but also thought about what he'd said to me and how he would've approved; how he would've been happy if he could've seen us and that.

And yeah... you know it sounds pretty stupid as I say it now, but I guess this was the start of me not feeling guilty any more for Colin not being there. I remember on this night, as I sat there on the beach with everyone, for the first time in ages I was feeling and thinking, well... like I was gonna be okay.

TWENTY

I have no idea of when we got up to go but I know it was late and we were completely fucked. We all, like the six of us, left together at the same time, splitting up into our respective directions once we'd gotten to the main road, with Duncan taking the same route as me.

Me and Duncan didn't talk much on the way back; I guess we were too stoned to bother. But when we got to Duncan's flat and I was about to say, "Bye," I remembered about seeing him walk off into the sun earlier that day (or the day before, depending on how you look at it) and asked him where he'd gone; what he'd done with his afternoon: turned out he'd just gone home and gone to sleep 'cause he was, "So fucked from working all week."

So yeah, I said to Duncan that I'd, "See you later," and carried on going and pretty soon was walking up my road, singing to myself again too. Although this time it was Patterson, *The Name Song*; which is well cool.

My mum's light was on as I turned into my house but when I got in everything was dark so I figured she must've just gone to the loo or something.

The kitchen was a bit of a mess. There was an empty packet of B&H on the table which I thought was weird 'cause my mum had given up smoking. And in the front room there was this stench of smoke and alcohol and even *I* wasn't allowed to smoke in there.

I remember wondering what the fuck had been going on. It seemed strange for my mum to have had someone over but it really did seem like this'd been the case at first. Even so, I could only see one glass in there, a tumbler, which I picked up and smelt, and it smelt of gin which my mum never drinks; she's always been more of a wine person.

Under a magazine on the coffee table was a bowl with shit loads of cigarette stubs in. And there was also a chocolate wrapper; like from one of those big bars of chocolate you break into pieces.

I remember I didn't know what the hell had been going on

and in my stoned state it seemed interesting, kinda fun to look around for more evidence so I searched for another glass before checking for an extra pair of shoes at the front door and then I was looking for more clues in the kitchen, although I found nothing else out of the ordinary. (I later discovered she'd lost her job that day and the state of the house had been the result of a cigarettes, alcohol and chocolate binge – although she never actually admitted this so I can't really say for sure; I just know she lost her job that day).

But anyway, so like the mood I was in when I got in to bed was all of like, I dunno, there was an unsolved puzzle eating away at me and I found it well difficult to get to sleep. And while at first I figured it was 'cause of my mum, as I lay awake for longer I started to feel that... well maybe that it could've been something else; I wasn't sure.

What I did know was everything had been fine before I'd got home and once I'd got in it'd all (like the state of the house) been kinda exciting, entertaining even; if only for a few minutes.

But as I tried to get to sleep that night there was definitely this feeling that something was wrong: something weird I hadn't noticed. Something I'd forgotten about or overlooked... And I couldn't place exactly what that something was.

*

I dreamt about waking up on the beach, looking at my watch to see it was one o'clock and Alex and Paul were standing over me. As I looked up Alex said, "Let's go," and then I was walking with them until suddenly we were up on the cliffs but like in the car park at the top and Paul's van was there and they were like, "We need your help," and pointing to the van and as I looked closer I could make out there was blood on the van, not loads of it, just little bits of dry blood on parts of the bumper and around the chassis.

And then I was scrubbing away at this dry blood using a

bucket of soapy water and one of those green and yellow sponges like the ones they use at Price-Savers which was really hard work and my arms were hurting while the whole time Alex and Paul were just standing over me not helping at all, just talking together, smoking and that.

The more I scrubbed away at the dried blood, the more it just wasn't coming off (typical of dreams I guess). I remember looking around wondering if there was any cleaning fluid or anything but when I asked Alex and Paul if they had any stuff to help make the job easier they both simply laughed, like what I'd said was really funny or something and carried on talking to each other, ignoring me again.

In the background I could hear the sound of a train approaching.

I turned around and Colin was there. He opened his mouth as if to say something but no words came out. Just a fizzing sound I remembered from somewhere…

*

I was woken up suddenly by my alarm: *Beep beep beep beep beep beep beep beep beep beep beep beep beep beep beep beep beep beep*…

It only seemed as if I'd been asleep a couple of minutes – and whereas when I'd gone to bed I'd felt as though I was gonna stay awake all night and not be able to sleep, now I felt like I could sleep all day. It was well difficult to even move. Although of course I knew I had to and after a while of lying there I managed to force myself to roll out of bed, get to my feet, grab my clothes off the floor and put them on. Then I kinda floated down the stairs into the kitchen, turned the kettle on, but after seeing the clock on the microwave realised I didn't even have time for tea so I downed a glass of milk instead, running out the house down the road to the bus shelter, cursing the Sunday bus system (only one every hour) as I did so.

When I got to the bus stop it was just past seven forty,

which was what time the bus was supposed to come. There was no one else there, which meant either I was the only one with something to do at that time in the morning or the bus had just gone.

Bracksea was like, dead. Hot as well. The windows of the houses opposite were glinting in the sun.

I remember saying, "It looks like we're in for another nice day," to myself; then, "Who the fuck goes shopping on a Sunday morning anyway?" (which was a sentence we always used to say at work) and laughing.

About ten minutes later I was still there, becoming more and more angry, wondering whether to get a taxi, walk home and phone in late, or even to think, "Fuck it," and phone in sick (yeah, the Sunday train system in Bracksea is even worse than the bus so this wasn't an option).

I lit up a cigarette, thinking it'd help but the first drag made me feel ill so I threw it away.

Can't remember anything else; I think my head was just empty. I know I was there for ages, that I rolled another cigarette to kick-start my brain into gear, which tasted like crap too but that I persisted this time, even though it was making me dizzy. And I remember my teeth feeling furry and I was wishing I'd remembered to brush them, getting pissed off about this.

But anyway, I was just about to walk back up the road home, my head struggling to function enough to enable me to make a definite decision as to what to do, when Bradby's car suddenly skidded into the bus stop out of nowhere.

The door burst open and it was all *boom boom boom boom boom* from the sub and Bradby was sitting there in his sunglasses holding and sort of studying his CD pouch, not looking at me but saying, "All right mate."

So yeah, feeling this sense of total relief I threw down my second half-cigarette of the day and got in, saying, "Cheers," to Bradby as I sat down next to him.

Still looking at the CD pouch Bradby asked if I fancied, "A bit of Mega Access," and I said, "Cool," even though I had no idea who the fuck Mega Access were; I simply felt happy to be in the car, no longer having to worry about getting to work.

Bradby put on the CD asking how I was doing and I said, "I feel like shit," and he said, "Me too mate."

Then, with the sound of Mega Access filling the car with a, I dunno, horrible noise to be honest, but kinda cool considering the situation (and it was totally waking me up at least), we sped off towards Skipton.

TWENTY-ONE

On the way there Bradby told me what'd happened the night before. He hadn't got arrested exactly, although he had got taken away in a police car. When I asked him he was like, "Nah, they just had a word," but admitted he was, "Shitting myself," at first. What'd actually ended up happening though was that they'd only taken him home.

It was interesting to hear Bradby talk about it 'cause he started telling me all about how they (there were two coppers) were, "Quite funny," and even said one of them was, "Cool," describing how he kept making sarcastic comments whenever he'd seen someone on the street, like slagging off all the piss heads and even the normal people as they drove past, which had been, "Funny to listen to." (Bradby did retell a couple of the jokes he'd made but I can't remember exactly; basically taking the Mickey out of people's appearances, behaviours and that).

So in the end he'd merely been taken home and when they got outside his house they told him they were gonna take him in to have a word with his parents but it turned out they were just winding him up, trying to scare him and, "Make me sweat," and in the end they just let him out.

I said to Bradby I reckoned if it had been me it would've been different and he said, "Yeah, I guess I was pretty lucky," and I said, "Luck doesn't come into it," and he was like, "What do you mean?" but I wasn't sure exactly what I did mean then so I just left it, saying, "Nothing," and after a short silence he came out with, "Yeah actually I was quite lucky 'cause my parents were asleep and didn't see the police car," and I said, "Yeah, my mum would've probably got up to go to the loo at that exact moment or something," and he laughed.

So anyway, we pulled in to the car park and as we walked towards the store I remember looking at my watch, noticing how late we were and saying, "Who's in charge today?" When he smiled and said, "Me," I wasn't sure how to take it although there was something about his tone of voice and the

81

fact he said nothing afterwards that put me at ease. Then he said, "So it should be an easy day," and it was like *cool!*

*

So by now I'd put the fact I hadn't being able to get to sleep the night before down to the state of the house when I'd got in, and actually it was a while before the whole Colin incident started affecting me again. But there's one more thing worth mentioning about this day, which is what Neale was going on about at lunchtime.

This particular Sunday was pretty easy, as me and Bradby had predicted. Not that we didn't work hard 'cause we did. But it was just nice not to have some manager, "On our backs the whole time." (Bradby was the one who'd said this and it was so true).

Anyway, at lunch I sat with Bradby and Neale, talking about the night before and for some reason I got on to the subject of how I'd woken up three times on the beach but that twice it'd been in a dream – I didn't wanna go into either of the dreams or anything, only saying how the first had involved four robots I'd previously seen on TV earlier that day and the other one had involved going up to the cliffs in Alex and Paul's van.

So what Neale said I can't exactly remember word for word but it was along the lines of how there was no way for certain for me to like completely be one-hundred percent definite as to which time it'd been real and which time it'd been in a dream.

I mean, when he was saying this to me and Bradby, we were like, "What?" and totally with no idea as to what he was going on about. Bradby was calling him a, "Ginger student," and it was actually quite funny 'cause the more we didn't understand the more Neale kept going at it, trying to get across his idea using different examples: of how the past is uncertain, the only thing we can be really sure about is the present and all stuff like this.

As I say, the more he went on the more we were laying into

him, how he was, "So full of shit." But it was still interesting enough to not forget and I guess that's why it stuck with me.

Even now as I think about his words... I dunno... a lot of what happened to me that summer I can't be totally sure about, and... yeah there's something in this idea that does give me a little comfort now. Just 'cause, well just 'cause it makes it easier for me to not worry too much about making sense of a lot of what I remember from the whole Colin incident.

TWENTY-TWO

So we were round Duncan's preparing to go out. I guess it was just like any other night, all of us round Duncan's again. Well, it was me, Graz, Neale, Duncan; and Bradby was possibly on his way. But it was indie night down The Basement and I was well looking forward to it. There was a bottle of red wine going round, Duncan was rolling like the fifth joint of the evening and everything was getting pretty funny.

We were all totally fucked. I remember, like clearly, lying on the sofa shouting comments to the others, feeling completely out of it. Graz was slumped in the wicker chair hugging his drink. Neale had just come well close to throwing up and at Duncan's suggestion was in the kitchen making toast. Even Duncan was looking pretty wasted.

We were trying to work out who we could call to give us a lift in to Firkinton 'cause Bradby had just phoned up saying his car needed to go in to the garage or something and we'd been relying on him for a lift.

It was a toss up between Dave from Skipton, who we hated, Ambra, who probably wouldn't come. Graz's friend Steve who we'd all never met: and apparently he hadn't phoned him for months. Alex and Paul, who were both pretty unreliable, and I was saying that Plant Pot from Price-Savers was always asking me to go out in Firkinton with him for a drink so we could call him: Duncan was taking the piss out of me, saying "You know that if we do phone him you're probably gonna have to shag him at the end of the night," and stuff like this.

There was this cool indie-hip-hop type music playing from a CD Alex and Paul had lent Duncan, which was well trippy and that as I remember, making my head spin; but in a good way if you know what I mean.

As I drew on the joint Duncan had just passed me I imagined the room as the dance-floor of The Basement, the fat DJ playing in the corner, the place full of fit indie girls, all wearing lacy dresses and corsets with loads of eye-liner and stuff.

Graz was going on about how the music was crap, with Duncan getting a bit defensive, saying things like, "Just 'cause it's not in the fucking music press right now," and, "You've gotta give it a chance."

The decision so far was that we were most likely gonna get the bus there: we'd finally got hold of Ambra's mum who'd said Ambra was already in Firkinton, could probably give us a lift back but could only take three of us. Bradby still hadn't turned up so we'd said, "Okay," secretly agreeing that if he did come then she couldn't turn one of us away if we were all standing there in front of her; and I'd said I didn't mind hiding in the boot anyway.

So we were still in Duncan's flat, half-heartedly psyching ourselves up for a long shit bus ride along the coast; the atmosphere having pretty much dwindled into any other Tuesday night.

I remember Neale was especially quiet by then. Eating his toast and looking around all like wary of everything, like an animal or something; like cats sometimes do when they eat I suppose, if you know what I mean.

When I shouted over to him, asking about his girlfriend, how it was going, he was like, "Okay." And when I inquired if it was "Just okay?" he said it was, "A bit annoying having to phone her all the time," and I replied, "Fuck that."

Duncan asked if I knew what Plant-Pot's number was and I said, "Fuck knows," and then, yeah Neale was suddenly brought to life again, spurting all this stuff about it being so typical of Bradby not to be there yet and how, "Since going full time he's turned into such a boring git," which I couldn't help agreeing on actually. Although when this started us all talking about how shit it'd be to do what he was doing and like how we all wanted to do something better with our lives, I did feel a bit sorry for Bradby and his situation; although I didn't say anything about this of course.

Graz was now saying he'd rather die than end up stuck in a, "Fucking supermarket in fucking Skipton," while Neale was all on about how he was, "So looking forward to university," which made me think again about what the fuck I was gonna do.

To be honest I started to feel a bit jealous, wondering too what the hell I was gonna say if any of them asked me what my plan was. Although when Duncan asked Neale about his girlfriend he said, "We're gonna see each other at weekends," and like how it was gonna be an effort but they'd make it work somehow: I remember thinking again, "Fuck that."

Then Duncan was going off on one about how he was gonna, "Move to Canada next year," and that he had a mate there who'd got his own business spraying cars and stuff; but we all just started taking the piss out of Duncan's, "Dodgy mates," which pissed him off a bit I could tell. Still pretty funny though.

Anyway, a while after this Graz was talking about the train, how easy it was to jump it and hide in the bogs, which started us off on a set of heated plans of how we were gonna run on just after the train stopped so the guard wouldn't see us amongst all the people getting off.

So we settled on the idea of the train and then we had about half an hour before we had to leave and it was at this point when Duncan said he had, "A brilliant idea," and ran into the kitchen before quickly returning with a giant bong none of us had ever seen before.

I remember him looking totally proud as he ran back in and I think that's why we all cracked up on his return.

About half an hour later we were sprinting down the road to the train station and it was well cold, someone was cursing the weather and the train was fucking moving and we weren't sure if it was coming in or going out. Graz nearly got run over, suddenly I had a stitch; Neale was complaining about Bradby and Duncan was saying, "Fuck, fuck, fuck!"

TWENTY-THREE

The others were in The Bowman and it was raining a bit, typical English summer. I was in a call box phoning up Bradby to see if he could be persuaded to take us to Firkinton in his brother's car (which Neale had just mentioned he'd been using to get to Price-Savers). But now he was saying he didn't wanna go out in Firkinton anymore 'cause of having work in the morning.

I was like, "Go on, you know it's gonna be a good night," and, "It's only once a month," and, "You could go straight to work and not sleep and sleep tomorrow," and all this, but Bradby was having none of it. He was all, "No way," and "I'm not going clubbing and that's that."

Although he did say he'd come out for a quick drink in Bracksea. And I guess that's when our plans for The Basement fell through on this night; which was more than just a bit of a disappointment for me: at least at first. Even so, when I walked back into The Bowman everyone seemed to be having a pretty good time and I must admit it wasn't long before I kinda forgot about indie night.

Neale, Duncan, and Graz were all sat at the table opposite the bar playing drinking games, which I love, so I made headway to get a pint in straight away.

We played the game where you have to pour part of your drink into the pint glass in the middle, toss a coin each to see who has to drink it. And as usual I kept hoping I'd lose so I'd get to drink more. It was well fun.

So, I was just considering getting up to buy my next pint when I noticed this group of girls sitting on the table opposite us who seemed to be talking about me. One of them kept looking over and turning back to her friends, at which point they'd all start staring and like giggling and all.

They were about our age, or maybe a bit younger. All of them pretty fit. All like well done up: make-up and stuff, dressed for clubbing, drinking wine, obviously pissed as fuck. And it was a while before I realised one of the girls was the one from Price-Savers. She was wearing a hat you see, like a woollen one (yeah, *woollen hat* but fashionable; a sort of turquoise colour) so I didn't recognise her straight away. When I saw her this bolt of electricity went through me. It was like, "Shit, it's her!"

Bradby walked in the pub at that moment, his tall figure coming into view behind the table of girls. As I looked up he met my eye, gesturing to see if I wanted a drink and then he was looking over my shoulder, pointing to the bar, obviously asking the same question to everyone else. And yeah, as I glanced over to the table again I made eye contact with one of the girls, not deliberately, it just happened. She turned her head back at Price-Savers-girl behind her and said something. They both looked over at me and it was like: *shit, what the fuck am I gonna do now?*

TWENTY-FOUR

So, it wasn't long before Bradby made a comment about how I'd been, "Gawking at the girl in the hat," and did I know her or something? Then everyone looked round and like the whole table of girls started giggling again.

Bradby had caught up pretty quick on the drinking game (he'd downed his first pint) and was really pissed too by then. He was leaning towards me saying, "Go on, get in there," and then falling back into his seat again. Neale was saying that I should go over and talk to them 'cause: "Fuck it, it's worth a try."

I began to realise he was right but this only made me feel even more nervous, butterflies in my stomach and all that. I mean, the thing was, I knew I should make a move and I'd regret it the next day if I didn't but it was like, I dunno, I didn't really wanna have an audience if you know what I mean.

I started saying I couldn't be bothered, that it wasn't worth it and how maybe I'd say something later but the others didn't pay any attention and continued egging it on. As I moved my eyes over to the girls again I remember really wanting to stay in the comfort of my own group but the more they went on at me the more they were becoming less of a comfort.

I tried saying stuff like: "Why should I have to make the first move?" and, "If she's interested she'll come over to us," and "Why is it the bloke who always has to do the chatting up?" and stuff. Then I was imagining what it'd be like if girls were the ones who came up to us and bought us drinks; and I tried to start a conversation about this but the others just weren't having any of it, saying, "Don't try to change the subject Chambers."

Duncan offered me his pint (which he'd just bought) if I went over and talked to her, which I guess was the start of me seriously considering it. Although when Graz said, "All you have to do is go over and say something and you'll be in," all I could help thinking was negative stuff like, *unless*

89

she isn't interested, and unless she says: *"What? Who are you? What are you talking about?"* and all stuff like this.

But Graz was now telling me if I didn't go over then he'd do it for me. And although that prospect didn't sound as bad to me as I think Graz expected it to sound, I suddenly thought, "Fuck it," ('cause I'd had enough) and picking up Duncan's pint I went over to the table full of girls.

I was really fucked by then. I just said, "Hello," sat down at their table and waited for them to say something. One of the girls (her name was Jo) introduced me to the Price-Savers-girl-in-hat who'd been looking at me. Her name was Holly. Jo said: "Holly thinks you're really horny," and like the whole table, except Holly, burst out into this cackle of laughter.

I responded with an, "Oh, right," and took a sip of Duncan's pint, wondering and like racking my brain for what else to say.

Jo then said, "So what's your name then?" and I said, "Everyone just calls me Chambers," which I thought sounded quite cool but Jo just came out with an, "Okay," like sarcastically and then, "Who's everyone?" and I thought for a bit before saying, "My mates," although even before I'd said this, she and the others had started talking about something which was suddenly more important and before I knew it I was caught up in this impossible-to-understand babble.

I tried to meet Holly's eye as I sat there and did for a moment and she smiled but that was it. All in all I was already starting to feel pissed off with my mates for talking me into this. So much for what Graz had said: I was pretty much getting nothing but a headache.

The headache got worse as they went on. I finally managed to tune in to part of their conversation when one of the girls was going on about how she'd met Dave Rupert back stage at a Sylvesta gig. How he was "So nice," and, "Really intelligent, he didn't say much but he'd always understand what you were talking about." – *Yeah, right*, I remember thinking and almost saying: *Whatever.*

Jo asked me what kind of music I was into; I said I liked indie and alternative stuff. Then Holly came out with telling me how she did too and that her favourite band was The Pearls - I thought, "Fucking great," but said nothing.

So yeah, suddenly I was sitting in the middle of all these crazy girls, all looking at me as if I was supposed to head up some conversation and how it was weird that I wasn't or something; but I just couldn't be bothered.

Although for some reason I didn't feel as awkward as I probably should've been feeling. Maybe it was the alcohol, I dunno. Now I think about it I reckon the fact I'd actually made it to the table at all was enough for me for the time being and I was merely sitting there satisfied I'd like done it and that.

I did wanna talk to Holly though. And I remember trying to think of all the things I could say to her: like, "Are you okay?" and "Which college do you go to?" and "Do you usually come out in Bracksea?" and, "I haven't seen you in here before," were coming to mind but then was feeling I didn't wanna get into any of that stuff. Also, as I said things in my head everything was sounding nothing but lame so actually, yeah, I think for ages the only thing I did say to Holly was I smiled and said, "All right?" And she looked shy which made me feel good, more relaxed.

After a while though one of her mates (not Jo, another one) said, "Why don't you say something to Holly?" (which was well annoying: just 'cause I wasn't all going at it with her! I remember thinking: *yeah see how you'd cope in this situation!*)

But I just said, "Sorry I'm a bit pissed," and they all laughed, including Holly this time.

The girl then said, "Don't worry, Holly is too." Then they all like burst out into this noise of laughter again.

TWENTY-FIVE

So I didn't think was getting anywhere, but after a while Holly's leg was touching mine.

At first I thought it might've been by accident or something; then when her foot started moving up and down my leg I suddenly got the horrible thought that maybe the foot didn't even belong to Holly at all. But I managed to catch her eye finally and she winked at me – yeah I thought this was pretty weird at first, but yeah, turned out Holly wasn't as shy as she seemed.

Anyway, like the next thing which happened was the bell rang for last orders and Jo was asking what people wanted to drink (although she didn't ask me) and then she was over at the bar; the other two girls suddenly got up to go to the loos together and I was left there with Holly.

Before I could say anything (which actually was quite a while; there was a bit of a silence at first) Holly came out with, "Do you remember me from Price-Savers?" to which I replied, "Yeah, of course," and then, "Do you remember me?" and she was like, "I had a job interview," and I said, "Really?" and, "When?" with her sort of looking at me funny and saying, "On Saturday," and I was like, "Right," and, "How did it go?" and she replied, "Shit," which made me kinda laugh.

And actually, before I knew it I was going into all these Price-Savers stories which she was finding pretty funny – just stuff about how slack I was, about the managers, Plant Pot and the trolley guy, Raver-Dave and Bog-Boy – and then she was telling me all about her interview, how badly it'd gone 'cause she'd said stuff like how she was only looking for something for a couple of months and also how she'd been scared of, "The weird, scary tall guy," interviewing her (who I guessed from her description to be Vader).

So it was kinda going all right, and yeah, it was hard to know exactly what the fuck was going on 'cause her foot was still moving up and down mine the whole time, but weirdly it was as if I was on autopilot or something.

Everything I was saying seemed to work.

It was a bit embarrassing though 'cause while we were chatting everyone (Bradby and Neale especially) kept looking at me as I was talking to her and making gestures at me; but she didn't notice or anything.

When the girls came back to the table we were quiet again, which was kinda annoying. But then all of a sudden Graz was standing there, all, "All right ladies?" which I was pretty happy about 'cause finally it gave them something else to focus on. Then he was asking if they were all going down 85s and they said that they were.

It was around this point when I realised how much I was dying for a piss. I remember looking at Graz, like willing him to get me away from them all.

He finally looked back at me in the end though and said, "How's it going?" and I said, "I'm dying for a piss," with everyone laughing and then I sort of struggled to my feet, (it was almost as though I'd been glued to the chair for the past however-long-it-was) and before I knew it they were all up too and then I'd hardly got a chance to say, "Bye," to Holly when they were all walking out the door; although Jo was sort of hanging back talking to Graz a bit but not for long.

When I came back from the bogs I headed straight back to the table where everyone had been but no one was sitting there any more.

I looked around and spotted Graz on the other side of the pub by the door talking to someone so I went over there. He was with a couple of blond girls, not really chatting them up, more talking I reckoned so I stood there for a while hoping to join in, but after a while realised I'd been standing there saying nothing for a little too long so I went off to find the others.

There weren't as many people in the pub by then, just the odd group finishing up, most of them standing about and getting their stuff and the bar staff were walking around clearing all the shit, telling people to, "Drink up."

I wandered towards the back of the pub to find Neale and Duncan coming out of the bogs. Neale was well pissed: he came up to me sort of stumbling, saying I was, "The fucking man," or something and then asked if I could, "Hook me up with one of her mates," before going on about how much of a, "Bitch," his girlfriend was.

Duncan said, "Don't worry about him man, he's wasted," and asked if I fancied, "Rolling one up," before we went to 85s. Then he suddenly pointed over at Bradby who was in the corner minesweeping all these drinks from one of the big tables over there. Neale started laughing hysterically, calling Bradby a, "Fucking scab!"

Bradby came over with three half empty drinks in his hand, asking me if I wanted one and I said, "Fuck yeah," and took the bluey-red one and downed it. Then this bar maid came up saying we had to go and Bradby and Neale started being lippy and that, and Bradby was saying, "How about one more drink?" and when she replied, "We're closing," he said, "How about we go upstairs then?" and we were all laughing and she was getting really pissed off.

So anyway, once we'd got outside it was still fucking raining so we kinda half ran half walked quickly towards the club.

On the way there we saw some townies trying to start a fight with a bunch of guys in our year (well, my, Bradby's and Neale's year) who we knew really couldn't handle it (they were proper nerdy and that). Bradby went over to put a stop to it, get involved, whatever, so me and Duncan took the chance to roll up.

We headed over to the bus shelter; skinned up there. I remember Neale was all like, "Give me some, give me some," and Duncan was saying, "Are you sure you can handle it?" and to be honest the state Neale was in he really wasn't gonna be able to but in the end me and Duncan just smoked most of it and it was almost at the end by the time I passed it to Neale: he was really starting to look more and more wasted though, sucking on the roach and that.

Yeah, and just before we got to the entrance of 85s I remember us trying to calm Neale down so the bouncers wouldn't notice how pissed he was. Duncan was like,

"Breathe," and I remember telling him to practice walking in a straight line. Then Bradby (who'd returned by then) was pretending to be a bouncer with us testing Neale on how he was gonna make his approach, asking him questions like, "Where's your ID?" and, "Have you been drinking tonight?" and, "Who are you with?"

The bouncers were all right though actually; they didn't check any of us. When we got there each of them so talking about something on their radios so we just walked straight through.

As usual it was packed. Fluorescent lights with the dark mass of bodies underneath. Everyone dancing to shite music, queue for the coats, queue for the bar. I remember there seemed to be some sort of theme going on that night too 'cause I immediately noticed there were loads of guys in suits and girls in angel costumes; maybe it was a party or something.

I couldn't see any sign of Holly though; not anywhere.

A group of fit looking angels pushed passed us and Duncan said, "Fuck me," to himself, then Bradby shouted, "Fuck me!" really loudly and like over to them, causing me and Neale to burst out laughing.

The four of us headed to the bar to get some drinks.

TWENTY-SIX

I ordered a pint of cider 'cause I wanted something that'd last and also get me more pissed. Neale and Duncan started trying to chat up the barmaid, but were doing it really badly, while Bradby and me were kinda standing away from them, pretending we didn't know who they were.

We stood there with our backs to the bar watching everyone in the club. I couldn't see any sign of Holly anywhere.

The music was this eighties song that'd been remixed by someone (I think some famous DJ) which everyone was always slagging off at the time saying that the original was better but I kinda liked this one 'cause it was faster; don't remember what it was called though.

I felt like going for a dance but I didn't wanna embarrass myself in front of Holly (wherever she was) so I was just kinda standing there for a while, thinking about what I could say to Bradby: I didn't really wanna talk about work, didn't know anything about cars, he wasn't into my type of music, he didn't really have girlfriends; he just *had girls* sometimes but never really talked about it and somehow we never asked him…

I was starting to wonder if the silence had been going on for a bit too long and was looking over to Neale and Duncan who were also saying nothing, when Bradby suddenly put his face close to my ear and shouted, "There she is," and I like followed his gaze to see Holly with all her friends in a circle on the dance floor, waving her hands and her hair around looking pretty wasted. And actually I remember wondering for a horrible moment if she cared or even remembered who I was.

I said to Bradby, "What do I do now?" and he said, "Do nothing mate, she'll come over in a while," which was easy for him to say 'cause come to think of it I'd never seen Bradby actually chat anyone up, it was always girls who came over to him. But I didn't exactly have his looks and like, physique, build, or whatever.

Neale came up then saying, "Go for it, it's now or never," and I looked back at the circle and they were all holding hands and I wondered again what the fuck I was gonna do.

Then Duncan came over and said that he wanted to get rid of his gear, saying about the bouncers who were still walking round talking on their radios and that, and asked if anyone fancied going back out with him for a bit. Bradby said I shouldn't 'cause it wouldn't help or something and then Neale started going on how he thought we should go up to start dancing with all the girls.

But when I looked back at Holly again I suddenly felt a bit pissed off for some reason. It was as though she was fine as she was and, like, no longer seemed to give a shit about me. So I downed my pint and followed Duncan back out.

We went round to the alleyway behind the club. Duncan said he'd been worried that the bouncers were, "Gonna start doing searches," or something and I said, "Right," and then, "Yeah," although I reckoned he was just being paranoid and it would've been okay.

But still, the fact that he wanted to get rid of his gear meant the joint he was now rolling was fucking packed. And 'cause of the mood I was suddenly in, this was more than fine by me; plus it was nice to be outside; have time to think and stuff.

Yeah, we didn't talk at all actually; we just smoked. But it was good to get back to reality again. I mean, it was like ever since sitting in that chair I'd been kinda absorbed into this, I dunno, plan or path or something which I hadn't even like chosen to step upon or be a part of but had somehow been unable to escape from; if this makes any sense.

At any rate, I actually remember being totally aware that 'cause I was now outside smoking a joint in the alleyway with Duncan, I'd got back to being in control again. At least that's the feeling I was getting: like it was now my choice whether anything was gonna happen with Holly or not. And it felt good.

Anyway, it was around this moment, while we were there in the alleyway – me thinking about all this stuff and Duncan thinking about whatever the hell he was thinking about; probably Canada or something – that we started to hear voices and before long could see the dark silhouettes of two bodies walking towards us.

It was Alex and Paul. They were each smoking a cigarette and Paul had a bottle of JD in his hand. As they saw us Alex said, "Hey, what's up dudes?" (the *dude* being a sarcastic expression) and Paul, looking up at the sky, which had cleared a bit, was like, "Fucking weather man, what the fuck's going on with this summer?" and then, "So what you guys doing?"

When I said we were in 85s they were both like, "What the hell you doing in there?" and Duncan was looking a bit embarrassed actually.

Alex said, "Haven't been there in years," and then Paul was, "Has it changed much?" and Duncan started describing how the new revamp was shit 'cause it didn't have the same atmosphere as before, with Alex replying how he couldn't imagine it being possible for it to be any worse than it'd been; and Duncan was all, "Well, yeah," and, "You've got a point."

Paul offered me some of the JD, which I'd been eyeing the whole time, and I took a swig; well nice.

So anyway Alex said that they were going up to the park, asked us if we wanted to come. Then Paul took out this big yellow plastic bag from his coat pocket (yeah it was the sheepskin coat again, which had deep pockets and the bag was actually quite big).

Me and Duncan were like, "What the hell's in there?" and Alex and Paul together said, "Gunpowder," all proud as though it was the greatest thing in the world to be carrying around in your pocket – actually I must admit at the time me and Duncan were both like, "Cooool!"

Then Alex explained that they'd, "Found this stash of it in Paul's garage," and how they were now going up to the park to, "Make a bomb."

The first thing I thought was, yeah how fucking cool it was now gonna be to go and make a bomb in the park with Alex and Paul but then remembered about Holly and, well I knew I had to go back in, not just 'cause I had to this time, it was 'cause... well shit as it was thinking about that circle of girls in the club, I knew I'd regret it if I didn't.

So Duncan of course had said, "Cool," and now his joint was being held by Alex and it was pretty obvious he was going with them. And I knew there'd probably be some sort of explanation needed for me not doing the same: but I didn't give any. Duncan started to but I managed to hint to him how I really didn't wanna go into any of it and he understood.

Feeling kinda confident from the effects of the joint I took one more swig of Paul's JD and simply said, "I'll see you guys later." Passing the bottle to Duncan I headed again towards the club entrance, all of a sudden finding myself walking back into 85s alone.

TWENTY-SEVEN

The music seemed pretty weird when I got back in; but in a cool way: kinda trippy and that. It was sort of like being in a movie; at least I remember feeling or pretending I was in a movie, strutting through the crowd, people dancing around me and stuff.

I headed straight for the middle of the dance floor and engulfed by the people around me I rolled a cigarette, thinking about how much cooler I was than any of the 85s crowd. Then I started to dance.

There was something about dancing after smoking a joint that I well loved. I closed my eyes and dragged on my cigarette letting myself get into it, not moving about too much; just swaying my body a bit.

I started to imagine I was in a film. Like how I was the star and the scene was where I was hiding from the bad guys, swallowed up in the crowd, dancing so as not to look conspicuous. But while the bad guys couldn't see me the camera was on me the whole time. The scene would've been edited cleverly with lots of different angles thrown together while the music played over the top.

Opening my eyes a couple of times I couldn't see Holly anywhere but I sort of hoped she'd see me.

After my cigarette finished though, I felt a bit different. The fantasy of my scene was dwindling away and then I wasn't really sure what to do with my hands while I was dancing. And while the music was still pretty nice I didn't wanna seem too enthusiastic 'cause it was only 85s after all. So I pushed my way out of the crowd and started looking around for anyone I knew.

With the state I was in and the lighting it was hard to see any more than a few feet ahead. I was sort of tunnelling my way towards the bar hoping I'd see someone on the way; but there was no joy.

I spotted Charlotte after a bit though, talking by the bar to a couple of people I didn't know, looking quite cool actually in these silver trousers and this weird colourful top which

100

looked quite sexy. And I nearly went up to say, "Hi," but didn't (actually she soon started getting off with one of he blokes she was talking to anyway).

My mouth was feeling a bit dry so I got this chocolate alcohol drink from the bar then, and, yeah I remember this distinctly 'cause it used up all my money and it all happened so quickly, like my money disappearing into the hands of the barmaid unexpectedly and it being too late for me to be able to do anything about it.

So anyway, with my back to the bar I was sipping this strange drink – trying not to finish it too quickly – studying the faces of everyone who came into focus, wondering where the hell my mates had all got to, but still trying to look cool; like I didn't care. But yeah, couldn't see anyone. So after finishing the drink and another cigarette I headed to the second, smaller bar out the back.

Neale called over to me once I got out there. He was sitting at a table by himself, looking a bit miserable. He pointed over to Bradby who was talking to some well fit bird in angel wings in the corner and as I got closer to Neale I said, "Yeah I know, he's a bastard isn't he?" and Neale was like, "How the fuck does he do that?" and I said, "Fuck knows."

I sat down at the table with Neale, nearly asking him what the hell was going on with his girlfriend but then I couldn't be arsed so I just asked if he'd seen Holly anywhere. Him replying, "Fuck her man," and then, when I didn't say anything back he said, "I don't know; I think she's gone."

Strangely I didn't really care about Holly anymore when he said this though. Actually I felt a bit more relaxed, like I didn't have to worry about second guessing what the hell Holly's agenda was and how it involved me. So I actually meant it when I said, "Oh well, never mind." I mean, we were all finally in 85s for the first time in ages and it wasn't the sort of night that happened very often. I said, "Fuck sitting here, let's go for a dance."

Neale was all like, "No I can't be bothered," but he got up anyway.

When we got back out there the *Malteasers* song was

playing and it was like, "Oh my God," but Neale started dancing anyway. We stood by the edge of the crowd and actually, yeah I remember Neale doing a few of the dance moves to the song which was quite funny.

Pretty soon I think the music started getting a bit cooler and anyway before long I remember thinking, "Fuck this," (like standing on the edge and all) and said to Neale how we should go further in.

*

So we'd come across Graz and some of his other mates after a while and were dancing with them. The *Rabbit* song was playing and we were all doing sarcastic dancing, like pretending we were really into it and it was well funny.

Anyway, this was when Holly and her mates suddenly came up to us and then we were all dancing together. Before too long me and Holly had got closer and closer and all of a sudden we were kissing; just out of nowhere.

It felt well good: we kissed for fucking ages. And it was only a matter of time before my hands were on her arse.

A couple of times I thought about what the hell we were gonna do once we stopped and wondered if I was gonna have to buy her a drink ('cause I didn't have enough money left) but most of the time I remember thinking about how fucking cool it was to be relaxing into a passionate kiss.

It's all a bit of a blur but basically we never made it to the bar and were still on the dance floor – like, hugging and that; totally wasted – when the lights came on (we were alone by then actually; no idea how long we'd been there).

Holly said she had to go and get her coat and I went with her. As I was waiting I took the chance to see if I could spot anyone around and remember seeing Graz leaving with Jo and he was winking at me but didn't come up to talk or anything. I scanned the club for Neale to see if he was okay or what he was doing but couldn't spot him anywhere.

Holly came back with her coat. Her hat was on again and she was looking pretty cute. Yeah I can still picture her

102

standing there now, looking up at me with big eyes and that, most of her hair back under her hat. While there was, feeling like a proper man, putting my arm around her shoulder, leading us out towards the exit.

Outside it was pretty crowded. Some lads arguing with a couple of bouncers to our left, another bouncer at the gate encouraging people to get the fuck home, everyone just sort of loitering about, some sitting down talking and smoking, some standing around saying goodbyes or planning what to do next.

Holly said, "So where have all your friends gone?" and I said, "I think they've all left me," and when she said, "Why?" I said, "I think they knew to," but she didn't say anything back and looked a bit confused. I remember just really wanting to kiss her again, but it was weird with the sudden like, lack of music and artificial lighting; everything was real again.

I said, "So where are all your friends?" and she said, "I think my friends have gone too," and I said, "Cool," and laughed; then wondered if this was really the best response.

I saw Bradby then, and the angel he'd been with before. They were getting off by the hedge and I was gonna ignore them but Holly saw me looking and said, "Isn't that your friend?" and I said, "Yeah," and then I was suddenly shouting out, "Bradby!" and wondering why the hell I'd done that.

It was all right though 'cause Bradby said something to the girl and then came up to us smiling and like, "All right guys?" asking me what I'd been up to.

Holly actually found this quite funny, like as I looked at her and then quickly back to Bradby, thinking how exactly to answer his question.

Bradby asked me, "What are you up to now?" and I said, "I dunno, what are you up to?" and Holly laughed again; this time I wasn't sure why; she was kinda swaying a bit, holding on to me for support.

Bradby looked at her, then back at me, saying he was probably just gonna go home but, "Rumour has it that there's something going on down the park," and then, when I waited for him to like elaborate or whatever he said, "At least, some people are going down there."

He then asked me if I'd seen Neale yet 'cause apparently he was looking for me. I replied how didn't have a clue where Neale was and, "When was the last time you saw him?" and Bradby was looking around saying, "He was here somewhere."

Holly then said, "So who are you then?" to Bradby and Bradby was like, "Bradby," and, "How' ya doing?" and suddenly Holly and Bradby were going into all this small talk bullshit.

As they chatted I looked around me. The crowd was starting to thin out, taxis were filling up. Neale was nowhere to be seen: I wondered if he'd gone up the park, and if Alex and Paul had actually managed to make a bomb yet. Although when I looked back at Holly and Bradby talking I realised I wasn't really in the mood to find out; I just wanted to kiss her again.

Then the angel suddenly appeared, looking pretty fit, taking Bradby's hand and saying, "I'm Isabel," and for some reason started to shake Holly's hand.

Bradby looked at us both, smiled again and said, "See you guys later." He put his arm around Isabel and then everyone was saying, "See ya," and they were walking off leaving us still standing there, two of the few people still remaining.

I didn't really know what to do then. I asked Holly if she wanted to come down the park with me but she said, "No," and she wanted to go home.

And I thought that was it but as she started to leave she said, "Aren't you coming then?"

TWENTY-EIGHT

Me and Holly walked up the road a bit; then stopped for a kiss.

It was different this time: more of a real kiss. Like two people putting their lips together to make each other feel good. Her tongue was all right in the back of my mouth. I remember it feeling small and hard, moving around and that.

A few people went past but there were no comments. Actually all in all it was pretty quiet and the feeling was like we were alone.

After a while I put my hand up her skirt a bit, but not too much 'cause we were on the street after all. Her hands were just moving around my lower back; she wasn't touching my arse or anything.

In between kissing we made this kind of ironic small talk. Like, "So what's your name?" and, "How old are you?" and, "Where do you go to college?" and, "What's your favourite colour?" – I don't remember which of us was like the instigator for this game but either way it was pretty sexy to ask this kinda question and before going straight into a snog.

Yeah it was also a good way to get past all that stuff too: she was seventeen, went to college in Firkinton, studied art, photography and social studies; loved all colours, hated dance music, didn't go to 85s very often…

It was like this perfect moment of kissing. Better than in the club. Although same as in the club it seemed like it was gonna go on forever. And the way it was finally broken was really weird.

Sounds crazy to say this now but basically as I remember it, some big guy came out of nowhere, pulled me off her and hit me over the head.

I didn't even have time to see what he looked like: he was just big; that's all I remember.

But the memory is strange. It's like I can see him walking up to me, almost like this hunched shadow turning into a figure, seeing us both there, pulling me away and then my body is dropping to the floor and darkness is like swallowing me up, or at least covering my body until I'm no longer visible (by that time the big guy is gone and actually Holly is hardly visible in any of this – it's just her hair and hat that makes her recognisable as I'm pulled away).

It's weird actually. As I'm thinking about it all now I'm starting to make a connection between this incident and the time when Charlotte tried to kiss me in the park. Like how both times I passed out when a girl I fancied was with me and we were basically getting it on. And I'm trying to think if Colin had anything against me doing what I was doing on either of those incidents, at either of those times.

But I'm unable to come up with any reason he might've had for being angry.

*

The dream I had while passed out I remember distinctly. It involved the four robots again: the red one, the blue one, the yellow one and the green one.

It was actually not so much a dream but two visions. That is, as I came to there were two images in my head. (I know, it's strange to think how in the few minutes or seconds – I never did find out exactly how long – of being passed out that I was able to dream much at all, but I'm simply telling it as it is and this really is what happened as far as I know).

So in the first of these two visions or images I could see the four robots sitting down, I think on stools, just sitting about chilling and chatting and stuff. Two of them smoking cigars, their bodies hunched over, leaning forward in relaxed postures, robot knees high in the air. And in front of them, like in front of the semi circle they were making, on a small patch of yellowy grass were the tiny figures of me and Colin - compared to the robots we were of miniature size.

What me and Colin were doing was hard to properly make out 'cause we were so small and it was the robots who were mainly in view. Although somehow I understood it was some kind of fighting competition, like Sumo wresting or something; you know, pushing each other out of a circle and

106

stuff. And the robots were sort of half watching us, half talking to each other but I got the feeling they were probably betting on who was gonna win.

Now I don't know how this scene exactly properly flowed into the next one but anyway the second picture I got was kinda similar but reversed. This time the floor was white and smooth and the robots were toys and a lot more basic in shape (quite chunky). They had wheels and me and Colin were manoeuvring them by remote control, racing them. As with the other image I was looking at myself from the outside; I should also say that Colin had his long hair back here as well.

I have and had no idea what to make of each of these images, but either way, Colin was winning both times and for some reason I wasn't really that bothered: it was almost as if I wanted him to beat me.

*

When I came round Holly had my head in her lap, asking if I was all right and what had happened.

That was when the visions were in my mind, it was at this moment.

I stared at them, like the two images for a while (they were kinda swirling into focus, first one then the other then the other again) before remembering Holly and then turning to look at her I said, "Sorry, what?" even though I knew pretty much what she'd just asked me. And she said again, "Are you okay?" and, "What happened?"

I was lying on the concrete path and 85s behind us was giving off enough light for me to see everything pretty clearly; but in a dim colour. There were a few people around still but not many, and it was a bit windy with the trees making a slight hushing sound. It was all quite peaceful to be honest, which was actually making me feel really sober: completely.

I looked again at Holly. Her hat was off, hair was all around her face, fallen forward and that, her eyes big and

107

staring through at me, looking sort of half worried, half drunk.

I suddenly remembered the big guy hitting me then and I said, "Who was that?" and she said, "Who?" and I said, "Your fucking boyfriend, your fucking dad, how the hell am I supposed to know?" Although I wasn't that angry I sort of shouted anyway 'cause my head was hurting and I felt disorientated I guess. I remember she was looking at me all confused and that.

At this point one of her friends walked by us out of nowhere and started laughing, calling Holly a "Slag." Then some others were there too, people I didn't know, but they all kinda went past and didn't stop.

Holly ignored them and started putting her fingers through my hair, smiling at me, like in a reassuring way as though I shouldn't worry about whatever it was that I was worrying about. She then said, "Have you got a girlfriend?" but I didn't answer her, I dunno why; I guess I was still confused about why the hell I'd just been hit over the head – but she really was looking as though she had no idea why I'd fallen over.

I started looking for my tobacco and when I found it I began rolling up a cigarette, still lying there.

Holly then said, "Because every time I seem to meet somebody I like I end up being chased off by his girlfriend." Then she said, almost to herself, "Girls don't really like me," and started laughing.

I sat up and lit my cigarette, looking at her, and although she was laughing, something about her expression told me that she still seemed to be waiting for my answer. I remember her eyes seemed to say that she really did care whether I had a girlfriend or not and I wondered if she really did like me, and like, *why*?

So anyway, I figured I wouldn't make any dumb jokes and there was no point in being angry so I simply said, "No, I don't have a girlfriend."

Holly stared at me and said, "Why not?" and I felt like saying, "Yeah it's as simple as that isn't it? Like all I've gotta do is walk up to some girl and say, "Do you wanna be my girlfriend?" and that's it, never mind all the rules, all the ways to behave, things you've gotta say, things you shouldn't say…"

But I just smiled and said, "I dunno."

*

I really wanted another joint then. But not by going to look for the others at the park. I just sort of wished we could've gone for a joint together and talked a bit.

Instead Holly was simply dragging me straight in the direction of wherever the hell her house was and not really speaking much.

Yeah, I remember she didn't seem to be the most talkative of girls then and at first it was making me a bit nervous actually. Although saying this, whenever I said something she always seemed to find it pretty funny.

Like when I said I enjoyed walking around when it was dark, and then when I revealed to her that one day I wanted to write a story about a guy who walks around in the dark every night and by day he's a normal office person and nobody knows his secret.

And when she said, "What's his secret?" and I said, "That he walks around in the dark," she found it hilarious.

I guess the more she didn't talk the more I talked (maybe she made me feel the need to, I dunno). And the more I continued to go on the more it became like, *bullshit* I guess. And pretty soon she wasn't responding much at all actually.

Thinking about our conversation now… I know I told her the thing about how I had no idea what to do once the summer was over and about the ultimatum my mum had recently given me (get a job by the end of the holidays or move out), and how I definitely didn't wanna stay at Price-Savers but wasn't sure what job I really, like wanted.

And with her still not reacting I explained how I couldn't be arsed with travelling or university 'cause of the money… but she didn't say much to this either.

I do remember she offered me one of her cigarettes after a while, which was really thin and I'd never smoked one like that before and when I asked her where she'd got it from she said it was, "From Hong Kong," which I thought was pretty cool. (It tasted basically like a menthol but the way it smoked was the same as a roll up).

Yeah, and I then told her how I didn't really think of myself as a smoker (which was actually still true at the time) but how I really liked cigarettes - and I remember she was like, "Don't you smoke roll ups?" and I said, "Whatever," and, "Same difference," and she was like, "Yeah." And when she said she only smoked when she drank I asked, "Really?" and she replied, "Actually, no," which made us both laugh.

By then we'd already gone past the town and had headed east (I know this 'cause of the direction of the sea) into a part of Bracksea which I didn't usually go to; although I'd had a paper-round in that area years before: big houses and that.

Thinking about how to describe the road we were on… the thing that struck me most was how like protected, or even fortified, all the houses seemed to be. All big walls and gates with the tops of houses visible from far away but when you were actually next to a house it was always trees or a wall blocking your view. A lot of the places were camouflaged in ivy too. And although the couple of cars I did see were all proper expensive looking and cool to look at, there weren't that many 'cause all the places seemed to have garages; actually there were no cars at all outside in the road.

Yeah, the road… There was this eerie gothic type feel to it, like how it was really long, wide, empty and stretching further than I could make out in the darkness. And with all the big houses and trees on either side… but maybe this was just me and the time of day, I dunno.

Anyway, a few minutes later it'd become pretty obvious (I guess 'cause we'd slowed down a bit) that this was the road Holly lived on and suddenly I was staring up at one of the really big houses and we'd gone through an iron gate and walking along a gravel drive. Holly was telling me not to

110

make any noise, which was really fucking difficult considering how every step I took sounded like a fucking smashing glass, or whatever, and it was like, *bloody hell...*

TWENTY-NINE

We went through another gate and then we were in her garden. There were dustbins and a barbecue, a trampoline, a big tree with a swing; and a pond that I could just about make out – there were big stones around it and to be honest I only guessed it was a pond (but I was right).

The back door, which was just past the dustbins, was open and we crept through into the kitchen, me still trying not to make any noise.

The place looked pretty nice. Smelt sort of like a garden centre: wooden stuff, dried flowers on the windowsill... old fashioned plates. Yeah, I dunno, it just had this certain feel to it which was like it was new and old at the same time. Cool though. And yeah, bit messy but I could tell her parents were probably rich.

Actually I remember the first thing I properly registered fully was the big wooden kitchen table, which was huge and well nice, with what looked like part of a model aeroplane on and a newspaper was spread out under it. I asked Holly if she had any brothers or sisters and she said she had, "An older brother at university." Then she was following my gaze to the table and like, "Oh, what you mean that?" and I said, "Yeah is it yours?" to which she laughed, replying, "Yeah my dad's a bit strange."

We walked through to the front room which had a huge TV and separates – I noticed a Mary Hefner LP propped up against a cabinet next to the separates and was gonna ask if I could try it out but then thought I'd better not.

Holly asked me to, "Wait here for a minute," and disappeared through another door the other side of the room so I sat down in one of the armchairs, looking around, thinking how it was actually pretty cool I hadn't gone in to Firkinton after all; how I'd never expected to be sitting somewhere like this at half-two in the morning; and how we would've been getting a taxi back by then, or getting a lift with Ambra.

Then I started thinking like if the whole time I was meant

112

to end up in Holly's house and maybe this was why we'd missed the train at the start of the night (yeah, maybe a bit philosophical, but Colin would've understood this).

The front room was pretty nice as far as front rooms go: lots of stuff to look at. Weird ornaments, random pictures on the wall, a bookshelf full of videos behind the TV, a cabinet that I guessed contained more LPs.

I really wanted to look around a bit closer actually, like poke about a little, but I also kinda wanted to be coolly sitting in the armchair when Holly came back in so I just sat there, after a while wondering if I should move over to the sofa so when she came back in she could sit next to me; although then I was worried that it might look a bit weird.

Finally Holly came back. She'd taken her coat off, her hair was down and I think it was then I noticed for the first time how sexy she was; or maybe it was that I realised all of a sudden what we were probably about to do and it was like, "Fucking hell," and, "Game on."

She said, "My parents are asleep but we still have to be quiet." And then she sat down on top of me and we started kissing again.

THIRTY

After we'd kissed for a bit Holly asked if I wanted anything to drink. I actually really didn't know what to say to this. I wasn't feeling particularly in the mood for a drink and had been kinda waiting for her to ask me to go upstairs or wherever. I must admit I'd been feeling a bit nervous while waiting for her in the front room by myself but now I was anything but.

I said, "I wouldn't mind a cup of tea," which I instantly regretted 'cause tea takes ages to make.

She got up off me and disappeared into the kitchen. I heard her filling up the kettle with water and then she was shouting, "How do you like your tea?" which sounded like a pretty funny thing to say and we both started laughing: and then remembering we were supposed to be being quiet our laughter kinda turned to suppressed laughter which was really hard to stop.

So anyway, when she came back with two mugs of tea a few minutes later I expected her to sit back on the armchair with me but instead she sat on the sofa and asked if I fancied watching a video, which I really didn't have any desire to do at all: I just wanted to go back to kissing again and hadn't even wanted tea in the first place. It was nearly three o'clock in the morning and I hadn't gone back to her place to watch a fucking video and like, *what the hell?*

I said, "Okay," and she laughed and said, "I'm sure you do," but I didn't laugh back 'cause I wasn't totally sure what she meant by this; like, was she intentionally being sarcastic?

She went over to the shelf, coming out with, "What kind of films do you like?" and I said, "Anything's okay as long as it's good," and she asked, kinda blankly, "What does *good* mean?" to which I replied, "I dunno."

I really wanted to piss then so I asked her where the loo was. If I was gonna have to sit down through a whole fucking film I figured I may as well go for a piss first and relax. All of a sudden I was starting to feel not only sober but pretty tired and a bit wound up.

I wasn't sure if Holly could tell what I was thinking but instead of taking me to the bathroom she just said, "It's through that door on the left but be quiet and don't flush it."

When I came back Holly was watching TV. I picked up my tea and sat down on the sofa, but not like close to her 'cause I'd decided I wasn't gonna play any fucking mind games or whatever 'cause I just couldn't be arsed. I was too tired to be second guessing stuff and if it happened it happened but if it didn't I wasn't gonna get frustrated about it (yeah, I'd thought about all this while in the bog).

She was flicking channels and although the TV was fucking cool, the actual television set that is, I couldn't see anything interesting enough to tell her to stop on. I sort of wanted to check out MTV but before I could ask her she picked up this *Friends* video and said, "Do you like *Friends*?"

I'm not sure if she could see the horror on my face or not but she started laughing again and said, "Just a couple of episodes," in a whiny voice, which actually made me smile a bit, 'cause it was cute, and I said, "Okay, if you promise to be a good girl," and rubbed her hair.

She smiled but didn't say anything and I wondered for a minute if what I'd said had sounded a bit wrong, but then before I knew it she'd put the video in, pressed *play* on the remote and was cuddling up to me. While there I was, sucked into the world of Joey talking to Chandler about some bird he'd slept with who he didn't wanna phone back, saying how if she called him then he didn't live there. And like all I could think about was: *Lucky fucking Joey...*

*

There was this one time when me and Colin were in Star Breaks, which is or at least was this cheesy nightclub in Firkinton. We were both around fifteen, sixteen then and it was one of those underage nights where they served nothing but coke and crap but at the time even though we knew it was shit it was still an all right place to go sometimes.

115

Anyway we were there this one night, sitting at a table by ourselves when these two older girls came and sat at the table, talking to us and that. One of them was a bit fat and like half decent looking and the other had a fit body but a big nose.

Big-nose-girl was basically chatting me up while fat-but-half-fit-girl was with Colin.

And the thing was, like this girl had such a big nose and I really wasn't interested and she was sort of a bit moody and townie too. The more I looked at half-decent-but-fat-girl the more I wished to hell that it'd been the other way around.

So what I did, I waited until we were all dancing (or at least when we were all dancing I was feeling the urgency to go through with my plan) and I leaned across to fat-but-fit-girl, whispering that Colin really fancied her mate – there'd been time in between for us to talk; actually Colin reckoned they were both, "Dogs."

What happened next was basically that Colin was dancing with big-nosed-but-fit-body-girl and then they were getting off and I was sort of standing next to half-fit-girl who suddenly had to go and talk to some of her other friends; leaving me dancing by myself feeling, well at first quite awkward but pretty soon kinda like shit actually. Until in the end I wandered off to the bar upstairs, sat on one of the seats by the balcony and every time I looked down at Colin and the fit-bodied-girl they were pulling.

Finally I managed to get possession of a bar stool and spent the rest of the night sitting there drinking straight cokes.

But I struck up a conversation with this girl who was there (not fit at all but good to talk to) that night which lasted about an hour. And yeah, all this stuff came out as I was talking to her. Like about how Colin was always the one who got everything and had to decide everything and how I'd spent pretty much my whole life living in his fucking shadow and being his fucking sidekick and how he fucking loved that: like pouring my heart out to her for ages and that, giving her loads of examples of how most of the time Colin basically had no respect for me whatsoever (which wasn't completely true I guess but I was well pissed and angry and just going off on one).

It was almost kicking out time when Colin found me. As he walked up to us the not-at-all-fit-but-good-to-talk-to-girl whispered, "Is that him?" and I didn't say anything. Like it's weird, 'cause before Colin approached I'd been filled with such anger and been so ready with all these things I was gonna say to him. But as Colin was suddenly there standing over me I remember this horrible feeling of guilt, as if he knew everything I'd been saying and it was like I was sinking into the seat and I felt no strength at all and I just wanted to disappear.

What Colin actually said then was, "You can't leave without me," but, at least what me and I think the good-to-talk-to-girl thought he said was, "You can't live without me."

It was like this bolt of electricity paralysed me for a moment when he said that. All I could do was simply watch as the girl said, "So who the fuck do you think you are Mr Big Stuff?" and Colin replied, "I'm your fucking dad."

*

When the video finished (four episodes) Holly was asleep and I was dying for a piss again. I somehow managed to get up without waking her and made it to the loo and back without disturbing her parents. It was getting light outside and I was feeling a bit more scared about them finding me there. I remember thinking, "What if her dad gets up early for work?"

Holly was stirring a bit when I got back to the living room, her red hair suddenly looking bigger than ever, and I woke her up by pushing her slightly a couple of times.

She said, "I've noticed you around," in a sleepy sort of voice and I wasn't sure if she was still dreaming. I pushed her a bit more and her eyes opened suddenly and she smiled and said, "You're really nice." And I didn't say anything.

I said, "It's getting light outside," and, "Maybe I'd better go."

Holly said, "Why?" and I replied, "What if your parents catch me here?" and she said, "Don't worry they're okay."

Somehow I didn't feel reassured in any way though. I remember at that moment all I wanted to do was just get the hell out of there.

Holly got up and took the two cups and went back into the kitchen; I heard her washing them up. She then came back in and taking my hand she was leading me out of the room, up the stairs, her saying; "It's too early to go home," and me wishing I wasn't feeling so sober.

Her bedroom was behind one of the four doors at the top of the stairs. It was huge. There were loads of soft toys on floor behind the bed, a desk with papers and folders on (and a big text book I remember but didn't see the title), some clothes on the floor on the other side of the room, a small TV on a shelf, a CD rack and huge stereo on top of a chest-of draws opposite the door; and there was a big poster of The Pearls as a kind of centre piece. I wondered why the hell we'd spent so long downstairs.

When we got in she said, "But I don't want any more funny business mister," and kinda quietly laughed again before throwing herself on the bed, pulling the covers over her body.

I remember standing there wondering what the fuck I was supposed to do then. But finally after a few seconds I walked over and collapsed onto the bed next to Holly.

THIRTY-ONE

There'd been plenty of time for thinking as I'd spent the last two days in bed: plenty of time to think about Colin stuff; plenty of time to think about Holly.

Yeah, Holly... the thing was, when I'd left that morning I'd forgotten to get her phone number. It'd been such a rush, like we'd woken up at the same time and she'd gone downstairs and come back up a few minutes later saying her parents had, "Left for work hours ago," but that her grandma was, "Due round any minute." And the way she said it I was imagining this scary old lady hitting me over the head with an umbrella or something so I'd like downed the tea she'd handed me and next thing she was ushering me out the door and actually it was only at the last minute that I remembered to kiss her goodbye.

And yeah, walking along her road and all the way home I was feeling quite pleased with myself about how it'd all gone and that, until later that night I was wondering whether it'd be a good idea to phone her or wait a couple of days and when I finally decided, "Fuck it," and that I'd give her a call I realised that I didn't actually have her number and it wasn't even that I'd lost it or anything: I'd failed to get it in the first place.

So this had all started me thinking about whether she really wanted to see me again at all or if she'd like planned it to turn out the way it did, and, well finally all these thoughts basically led to me deciding to not let it get to me; which had taken a couple of days to properly accept. But by now I'd decided that if it was gonna happen it was gonna happen and if it wasn't then at least the night (which I'd replayed in my head pretty much a hundred times by then) had been a good one.

So, it was a Tuesday and my third day of doing practically nothing and my mum had been going on for long enough for me to reckon that it was worth heading down the corner shop to get the job section supplement. She'd managed to get a job already you see, and although it was only in Outlets, which was the shittest job I could possibly imagine doing, it'd given her all the ammunition she'd needed for her argument that it was, "About time you started sorting *yourself* out."

It was sunny again: had been for the last couple of days. And there I was trying to *sort myself out*, making my way down the road, across the intersection, into the corner shop, buying tobacco, a box of matches (my lighter had gone missing the night I'd met Holly), an *NME* and *The Daily Argus*.

I'd been pretty tired that morning and I remember it was kinda making me dizzy being out the house for the first time in ages. But it was nice, sun shining and that.

As I came out the newsagents I thought about going down the beach to sit there actually. Just to stay outside and go through the job section in the sun. It was summer and I knew there'd be loads of people there, lazing around, listening to music and just generally chilling out. And I really was about to go down there too, maybe even have a look for Graz and that. But the thing was, it was pretty hot and I reckoned that looking at the job pages in the full heat of the sun I wouldn't be able to concentrate (even if I didn't find Graz). I was frightened I'd only end up falling asleep or something.

I was pretty hungry as well, so yeah I headed back up my road with the intention of maybe going to the beach after some lunch, taking a drink and maybe a hat with me. My mum had shouted about, "Some chicken in the fridge," before she'd left for work, which I'd had a look at earlier on but hadn't been able to stomach 'cause it'd been one of those shitty pre-cooked ones from Price-Savers. There'd been loads of oil and fat swishing around at the bottom and it'd been a bit too early to start eating it but now I was feeling… well my mouth was now sort of watering at the thought of it actually.

I headed back towards my road, my hunger getting stronger as I started forming this picture in my mind of the people in the houses around me tucking into their lunches; imagining them to be feasting on all this amazing food: although then I was remembering that everyone would probably be at work and most of the houses were most likely empty. Which I guess led me on to looking at my watch and realising how it was first lunch at Price-Savers and I thought about sitting there with Bradby and Neale, eating whatever they were serving this time; could've been anything.

So yeah, anyway for some reason as I got to the junction I suddenly realised that I really didn't wanna go back home. I mean I still wanted the chicken and all but seeing the bottom of my road come into view... I just couldn't face being inside those walls again I guess. I mean, I'd spent the last three days trapped in that fucking place after all and the thought of going back in, I dunno, it just felt totally depressing all of a sudden.

I looked over to High Lanes and half considered going there. Then thought better of it and decided to try Duncan's instead. Strangely I had a feeling he might be in.

THIRTY-TWO

Duncan wasn't in. I wondered why the hell I'd expected him to be. I knew he was working. It was a Tuesday and everyone was working.

I knocked for a while though, calling his name and that. Then I looked at my watch – it was almost two o'clock; he usually got back at around six or seven – and thought about whether it'd be okay to break in, 'cause the window was always unlatched. But I didn't. I just sat on the doorstep instead and rolled a fag.

One of the houses opposite had some building work going on in the garden, there was music (fucking daytime Radio One shite) coming from it, filling up the whole close with background noise.

A couple of seagulls flew by the house as I watched, seemingly interested in what was going on. I lit up a fresh cigarette, staring down at the two papers in my hand, my stomach rumbling...

Then out of nowhere Colin was behind me saying, "You look lost Chambers."

He had his long hair back this time and was wearing his Leaters jacket. His expression was sort of smug, like he was relishing in the fact that he'd just me caught me unaware; I hadn't been expecting to see him after all and I guess he felt like he was giving me a happy surprise or something.

But he was wrong, 'cause yeah, unlike the other times I'd met Colin when I reckon I actually wanted to see him, on this occasion I had no desire at all for Colin to be standing there in front of me. I just wanted to be alone you see. The job pages I was gonna go through first and reading the *NME* would be my reward: the only thing I'd been confused about was where to go to find a place I could be comfortably by myself.

Now Colin was suddenly standing opposite me looking at me as if to say, "Now I'm here," and, "Are you ready?" as though I was supposed to drop everything and go with him.

I said, "Bloody hell," and then, "All right Colin, how's it

122

going?" and then I said again, after a pause of silence, "How're you doing?" my mind swirling and that, wondering like how or if I could get rid of him.

Colin was just looking at the papers in my hand though, stationary and not going anywhere. Then gesturing his gaze towards the *Argus* he came out with a, "What's that?" and I said, "Nothing, just my mum. She wants me to get a job," and he said, "Why?" and I was like, "Fuck knows," and laughing and that.

And yeah, Colin was then looking up at the sun and saying, "Where's Duncan?" and I said, "At work I guess," to which he replied, "Who the hell needs a job on a day like this man?" and I laughed a bit more and said, "Yeah."

The two seagulls flew past again, still scouting around for whatever the hell they were looking for.

"Probably out for a fight with some crows," I said to Colin, pointing towards them and he looked over behind him and said, "Fucking vermin, eh?"

*

Colin said he wanted to go down the beach but I said that I didn't and that it was, "Too hot down there," which took him aback a bit I could tell 'cause he like stopped for a minute before saying, "What do you wanna do then?" and I said, "I dunno," and then he was like, "How about we head into town?" and I couldn't think of a better idea so I said, "Okay."

We walked along the path by the main road until we got to the town centre and ended up in a café (I guess 'cause I was still hungry) – some café called Blacks and I'd never been there before.

The café was one of those old Victorian style (or at least it had an old fashioned look to it) buildings from the outside, as are a few of the places in Bracksea town. The doors were modern enough though and inside it was pretty ordinary and what you'd expect from a café in Bracksea: flowers and placemats on each table, nice warm smell and feel to it, playing this safe music, although it was at low volume; actually you could hardly hear it: but yeah, not exactly a trendy Firkinton café. Much more the sort of place your grandparents would love.

I remember it was weird us queuing up in a place like that, looking at all the cakes on display, then up at the menu behind the heads of the two cashiers (a man and a woman), wondering what to buy: Colin of course couldn't order anything 'cause he was dead and therefore wasn't able to eat but I was pretty hungry and ordered a toasted ham and cheese sandwich, a cappuccino and a slice of chocolate cake.

We went and sat down – me with my coffee and cake which I wasn't gonna touch until the sandwich had come and was finished – Colin looking at me as though by choosing to come to a café I'd somehow done something funny or something; although he wasn't smiling or laughing, it was just a sort of amused expression he was giving me.

I said, "We never did go to a café did we?" and he looked around (actually the only company we had were just a couple of old people sat at a table the other side) and answered, "Yeah, I'm not surprised."

But I carried on, saying, "I think they're kinda cool," and when he said, "What?" I replied, "Cafés." He was like, "Why?" and I said, "Just the atmosphere and that," and he was looking around again (I dunno, just simple wooden tables and the pictures on the walls were all of scenery of Banterbury county and that) and like, "Atmosphere?" But I continued trying to convince him, coming out with, "Yeah," and then, "Okay, maybe not this café but there's something about them that I've always kinda liked." And then I thought for a bit more before saying, "You know, like on the inside of the Kews album, where they're all in a café."

But Colin just said, like dismissively, "I thought that was a pub."

A waitress came up with my toasted sandwich: young and wearing a black and white, kinda sexy uniform. She put the plate down mumbling, "Enjoy your meal," and as she walked away I watched her before looking back at Colin, saying, "Pretty fit, ha?" with him giving me a, "Yeah, if you like that sort of thing."

The sandwich had burst; cheese and oil were oozing all over the plate; luckily I had a knife and fork though.

I said to Colin, as I started eating, "You can have some if you want," but Colin was like, "No, it's okay," and then, "Pass me the *NME*." I passed it to him and he opened it up and started scouring the pages, reading as though he was hungry for words not food.

After a while he looked up and said, "I didn't know Suntory had a new bass player," and I said, "Yeah, it's a bloke," and he said, "Poor bastard," and I laughed.

Then he was flicking through again, coming out with the odd quotation as I ate.

THIRTY-THREE

I'd finished my sandwich already and was half way through the chocolate cake. I remember it was rich and kinda rubbery and I was cursing the fact I'd run out of coffee first.

"Everywhere you go you get beer and drugs for free, girls scream at you and you feel like shit, but it's good," Colin was now saying, looking for my reaction and I said, "Yeah," and then, "Tell me about it," and he said, "Fuckin' nuts man."

He was still absorbed in the *NME*, his finger moving through the paragraphs of a Nictane interview with this sort of slightly disturbing enthusiasm: disturbing 'cause in the final few months of when he'd been alive he'd lost interest in all that stuff; I guess it was kinda strange to see him back to being so keen about it all.

"They've got a new album coming out soon," I said, and he was like, "Really?" and, "Oh man," which made me feel a bit guilty actually; or like sorry for him or whatever – but there wasn't exactly anything I could do was there?

I stuffed the last bit of cake in my mouth and pushed the plate away towards Colin, him mumbling, "No thanks," without looking up and then I said, "Do you wanna get out of here?" and he said, "And go where?"

I remembered about the job supplement then and said, "I'm supposed to be trying to get a job," and he... yeah he merely had another quote for me when I said this, saying, "I only went there because one of the awards I was up for was voted for by the people," and then we were both like, "Yeah, right!" at the same time.

Colin then looked up at me, coming out with, "So you're really gonna get a job then?" and I said, "Yeah, well, that's what you're supposed to do isn't it?" and he laughed and replied, "Fuck that man."

*

So it was a while later when Colin had come up with, "A

great idea."

We'd been sitting there half looking around, half looking down at the *NME* pages, avoiding too much eye contact – 'cause of both being blokes I suppose – and the wooden chairs weren't feeling quite as comfortable as they'd felt when I'd first sat down and there'd been a bit of silence for a while. I'd thought about telling Colin about Holly but hadn't: maybe 'cause of the mood I was in or the fact that I hadn't really been planning to see him. Or maybe 'cause of how he'd dismissed my opinion on how the waitress was fit; I dunno.

But yeah, Colin had come up with an idea. Which was a bit of a strange and random spot of inspiration 'cause the plan he came up with was that we were gonna get Alex and Paul to help me find a job. A pretty stupid plan now I think about it but at the time it seemed like something to do so I'd decided on going along with it. They were the oldest people we knew you see and we wanted to ask them... well, I dunno, we just wanted to ask them to tell us something useful I guess. What it'd been like for them, leaving college and all. Or rather what it had been like for everyone else when they'd been our age.

We got up and got our shit together and then I walked over to pay while Colin waited for me outside.

The lady behind the counter asked me to, "Wait a moment," and walked out into what I assumed to be the kitchen area, coming back a few minutes later with the receipt on a small brown dish.

It was handwritten and said: *Toasted Cheese and Ham Sandwich (1) - £2.75, Medium Cappuccino (1) - 80p, Chocolate gateau (1) - 90p*

The bill came to four pounds forty-five. I took the receipt and put a five pound note on the tray, gave it back to her, turned around and walked out. All like in a good mood all of a sudden, ready to go on a mission.

But when I got outside Colin had gone.

THIRTY-FOUR

It's funny. It's just as I hadn't expected him to appear when he did that day, I totally wasn't expecting Colin to disappear, or to have disappeared when I got outside. Although actually, saying this, once it sunk in that he wasn't there any more I realised how of course it was obvious (or at least it suddenly seemed clear to me) that this was the moment he was gonna choose to leave.

I looked around to make sure he'd gone, like up and down the street but there was no sign of him. Just Bracksea high street on a Thursday afternoon; a couple of old people and that was about it.

So I stood there, wondering what the hell to do, then thought... yeah I actually walked over to a phone box and was all ready to give Alex a call but then couldn't be arsed so I didn't bother.

I headed back to Duncan's instead. Dunno why. Guess I'd been considering the idea of breaking in just before Colin had appeared. Now that he was gone I suppose going back to where I'd been before seemed like the easiest or most like, logical thing to do. (I half considered giving Duncan a call just to check it was okay but I wasn't really up for disturbing him at work and I reckoned it'd be all right anyway so I didn't).

Having no walkman with me made the walk back there pretty dull to be honest, nothing worth mentioning. Although when I got to the top of Duncan's street I saw Charlotte on the other side of the main road waiting at the bus stop and I waved and then she waved back all enthusiastically; but that was it.

Duncan's window moved up with a bit of effort but I'd done it before so I knew what to do. The trick was to stretch to hold the left and right of it and to force it up quickly with an even pressure on both sides. This way it wouldn't make too much noise and there was no like shedding of blood required, or whatever (I'd cut my hand on Duncan's window once before).

So yeah, the first thing I noticed when I got in was how bad the smell was: sort of like how your bedroom reeks of the inside of your lungs when you wake up: and just generally seeing the place in daytime made it seem a lot more like a tip than it did in the evening. Something about the cold light of day, I dunno. But yeah, crap everywhere and that. A million unwashed plates and cups with mould in, ashtrays overflowing…

So I left the window open, which I figured would be a good idea anyway 'cause I sort of wanted Duncan to know someone was in when he got back.

I played *Monkey Warriors* first. The case had been lying on the sofa when I'd got in and I hadn't played it for ages so I thought like, "Why not have a quick game?"

I played that for a while, taking my time to kill all the little monkeys rather than saving my energy for the generals, which was more fun 'cause I always lost to the generals anyway. And I made myself some tea too. I did have a look for something to eat but there was nothing in the fridge worth eating apart from a snickers bar that I actually quite wanted but I reckoned nicking Duncan's snickers might've been going a bit far. (And also of course I made a quick search to see if there was any gear lying around but there wasn't).

I went back to *Monkey Warriors* with my tea and had a few fags, killing time and all the monkeys; not really progressing that far in the game. Even so, it was around six, seven o'clock when I'd finally had enough: I totally hadn't been keeping track of the time and it was a bit of a shock when I realised like how late it was and how long I'd been there and that.

My eyes moved to the two papers on the sofa next to me and my head started spinning (probably from staring at the TV screen for too long; there were little monkeys running all over the room). So I looked around thinking about what else there was to do, wondering like when the hell Duncan was gonna get back.

The curtains had come apart at the top a bit letting in light from the streetlamp outside and I thought about seeing if I could repair that just to occupy myself for a bit but then I couldn't really be bothered. And also I half considered giving the place a bit of a tidy but then came to my senses again and I was saying, "Fuck that," and laughing.

The cat in the picture stared at me as if to say, "What the fuck are you doing here Chambers?" and I remember thinking, "Yeah, what the fuck am I doing here?" and laughing even more.

Then I noticed a bit of weed on the floor. Just like a tiny bit. But it gave me a cool idea and I decided to see how much of it I could get off the carpet, thinking also that there was most likely gonna be shit loads in the sofa.

I fell off from where I was sitting and crawled over to the stereo first to put on a CD though. I'd been wanting to put on some music for a while 'cause, yeah Duncan had quite a cool collection to choose from and I'd just been waiting for the excuse. Dunno why but with nothing to do just lying there and listening to music felt more like I was intruding than it did if I was listening to music and doing something at the same time.

Anyway, when I got there I noticed how much all of Duncan's CDs had grown since the last time I'd properly had a look and it was like, *cool*.

Although the problem was they weren't in any order or anything. Actually it was kinda annoying, especially as, yeah they weren't even in the right cases too. I remember deciding on a Shine CD finally 'cause it had a few good tracks on but then when I opened it there was a Long Life Mild CD inside and I was looking around for Shine, opening all the cases but wasn't able to find it for looking and it was getting more and more frustrating; I guess 'cause it was well difficult to stop searching.

Finally I managed to like give up the chase though and settled on a Kews album which was the CD that was in the player and had been the whole time. And once the music was on I felt a bit more calm again I suppose.

After that, well actually it was quite fun looking around on the floor for gear. I got a saucer from the kitchen and was putting all the bits on there. By the time I'd finished with the sofa (I took the cushions out and found a pretty reasonably sized clump in there which helped a lot) I'd accumulated enough for a joint.

So there I was moving my feet up onto the couch to make myself comfortable. I got one of the pillows from the floor and put it behind my head and then, with my papers and backy on my stomach, dish of gear beside me and The Kews in the background I went through the familiar routine of rolling up.

Pretty soon I was asleep.

THIRTY-FIVE

What I dreamt about I have no idea but when I awoke I was wet through with sweat. My T-shirt was stuck to me and it'd twisted out of position. My backy pouch had somehow opened up and there was tobacco everywhere.

As I turned over Duncan came into focus, sitting in the wicker chair, his hair down smoking a joint; I had no idea how long he'd been there.

He was like, "Are you okay man?" and I said, "Yeah," wondering what he meant by this and if I'd been tossing and turning or something but he didn't say anything more… apart from he did ask me who Holly was a few minutes later and I laughed and said that she was, "The girl I met the other night," and he said, "Oh," and then sort of looked away.

And then when I asked why he hadn't woken me up he said he'd been a bit scared to 'cause he was saying that, "It's not a good idea to wake someone up when they're dreaming," 'cause they might die or something and was telling me about this thing that he'd read once about this happening and I remember asking him how anyone had known the person had been dreaming and he said, "It's easy to tell," but didn't like elaborate or anything.

So of course I had to explain to Duncan what I was doing there in his flat but it was pretty easy 'cause I simply said I'd, "Had an argument with my mum," and he said, "Don't worry about it," and that was it really.

There was no music on in the room, it was silent. I looked around before asking Duncan, "What's up?" 'cause, I dunno, just the way he was sitting, not saying anything and how he'd hardly shown any reaction to me being there. I knew he wouldn't mind but I still thought he would've said a little bit more in response to me lying asleep on his sofa when he'd got in.

He said, "Nothing man," and then I said, "How come you're back so late?" and he said, "I had to go see my dealer."

He offered me the joint then and I sat up and took it, asking him, "So how was work?" and he said, "I no longer have work," and then looking over towards the TV asked me if I'd, "Fancy a game of *Monkey Warriors*?"

*

So we played *Monkey Warriors* and Duncan told me all about how he'd walked out of his job.

We'd all known for ages about how much Duncan didn't get on with his boss and had listened to it enough times. Like how he thought his boss was a twat who was, "Under the impression he's better than everyone else," and walked around all day saying things to the employees like... I dunno, just annoying stuff I suppose and you kinda got this picture of a guy with a stick up his own arse pissing everyone off and that.

Duncan though was often telling us stories of how he always used to confront his boss and give advice and point out stuff to help him do his job better – to be honest I actually have and had no idea what Duncan's job was. I mean, I know it was at SAMPOs which was some kind of workshop but I don't really know the exact situation or what they made or repaired or whatever – and it was obvious that the guy probably hated the fact that Duncan knew more about his job than he did; despite Duncan's appearance and age and all. Or maybe Duncan just wound him up, I dunno.

But anyway, this time Duncan told me that an argument between them had ended up in him walking out.

So now he was with me killing just as many of the little monkeys as I was, all like eyes focused on the game with his mind obviously somewhere else with me just humouring him, and it was sort of frightening a bit actually. The way he was obviously so angry and not showing it and that.

Anyway, we defeated the first general and then Duncan suddenly paused the game and asked me if I wanted some tea and I said, "Cool." And when he came back from the kitchen he said that he couldn't, "Be arsed with any more *Monkey Warriors*," and walked over to the stereo asking if I fancied, "A bit of tunage."

I lay back on the sofa thinking about what I could ask him to put on, trying to remember what I'd seen previously before then deciding that I didn't really care. And before I had the chance to tell him this he turned to me and said, "How about a bit of drum and bass?" and I said, "Cool."

*

It was a couple more joints later when Duncan started talking. Telling me in detail about how he'd been working on this machine for cutting wood that'd broken down or something and basically he'd fixed it and it was working well, better than it had been before and it'd been like a, "Proper big job," and a, "Good morning's work," so when he'd finished he'd chosen to take an early lunch.

When he'd come back from lunch though his boss – Duncan told me, "My boss's name is Jim," – had been all like, "Duncan can I have a word with you?" and had taken Duncan into his office and shouted to him about how, "We don't go to lunch until we've finished the job!" and Duncan had been like, "I did," and then according to Duncan, "Jim was sort of giving this confused look as he was thinking of what to say next," and Duncan had told him, "I'll show you if you want," and Jim had said, "Okay, show me," and Duncan had then led him to the warehouse where the machine was and then apparently Jim was sort of looking at it for a long time, testing it and that, and then said… I dunno, something about how a part was missing or something, but anyway Duncan had been like, "Yeah the reason for this is that it spoils the rotation," and how whatever was missing wasn't necessary and, "I think you'll find it was [the missing part] that led to the problem in the first place." But Jim had said, "This is not the way you were supposed to do it," and although Duncan had told him, "If you just have a look you'll see that it works a lot better now," Jim had been like, "I want you to do this again the way you should've done," which Duncan told me meant taking the whole thing apart

134

and starting again from scratch.

So basically Duncan had said, "If you really want me to change it then I will but I don't think it's a good idea, and it's not gonna work as well," and Jim had been all not knowing what to say again; although he probably knew Duncan was right and that.

But what happened next was Jim had said to Duncan that he was docking his pay 'cause he'd gone for lunch without finishing the job properly and Duncan had been like, "If you dock my pay then I'm walking out," and Jim had said, "Fine, go then," (or something like this) and then Duncan had basically gone and got his stuff and left.

THIRTY-SIX

While Duncan was telling me all of this I'd been formulating a plan in my head, which I reckon had arisen from my feeling the need to cheer Duncan up.

When he finished talking I said, "Fuck that man," and, "Who the hell needs to work in a place like that anyway?" and, "You really shouldn't have to put up with that shit," and stuff like this. And yeah I agreed with him about how he hadn't done anything wrong as I guess I was supposed to.

But it was then, as he finished and we were sharing some silence again that I finally had the chance to say what was really on my mind, saying, "So you don't have work tomorrow," and he was like, "That's true," and I said, "We should go out," and then he looked up at me and said, "Okay," and it was like, *cool*.

My mind started working away, thinking about all the possibilities there now were. Going out in Bracksea, maybe a pub crawl... I was also thinking about Firkinton too. There were plenty of things to do there.

Duncan got up and went over to the cabinet under the TV and got out this dusty brown bottle and I said, "What's that?" and he was like, "I got this from my uncle," and I said again, "What is it?" and he replied, "Rum," and, "I'd been saving this for a special occasion."

He then went into the kitchen, coming back with two small tumblers and opening up the bottle he poured us both a decent measure. There we were saying, "Cheers," and clinking our glasses and sipping the stuff, kinda tentatively at first – yeah I remember like even though it tasted pretty harsh I said, "Nice," to Duncan and he took a bigger swig and said, "Man this stuff tastes like shit doesn't it?" and I said, "Yeah," and downed what I had left, asking for some more.

So we persisted with the rum. And a couple of conversations and refills later we'd changed the music to the *Farewell Sally* soundtrack and the atmosphere in the room had lifted. Duncan was all on about travelling again, except this time it was to Japan 'cause he'd known a mate of his brother's who'd gone out there teaching in Tokyo and apparently it was a well cool place and the girls were proper fit and that.

And he was saying about how no one really smoked gear there and how he really wanted to go somewhere where people didn't smoke gear all the time and was all, "Better not," about Thailand when I'd said about how it was supposed to be well cheap out there and how Thai girls were meant to be fit as well and that.

It was around a third of the way through the bottle when we started actually planning where we were gonna go and what to do. Duncan was kinda short on ideas actually and was leaving it up to me: my thinking was that we should phone a couple of people first, get them round and then see what everyone thought.

I went over to the phone while Duncan moved to the armchair and started to roll up a joint; we needed a break from the rum.

So Duncan was sitting opposite me as I made the phone calls. Telling me what to say and letting me know the numbers while I did the phone. (Yeah he seemed to know everyone's number by heart, even mine!)

We tried Neale first. He was the most likely to be up for it we reckoned. And at first he seemed to be totally cool with the idea. All like, "Yeah, could do," and asking us what we had planned. But when I then said, "Nothing so far," but that we were, "Probably gonna go in to Firkinton," and, "Just get round Duncan's and we'll go from there," I could tell he wasn't sure all of a sudden, and… well I guess I wasn't persuasive enough or something (actually I was holding on to the phone not saying anything for ages too) and he then said, "I've got Laura round," and I guess that's when I realised that maybe getting Neale to come out was gonna be harder than I'd bet on it being.

But I answered, "Oh right," and then, "Well she can come too," and when he replied, "She's got work tomorrow," I did suggest how he could, "See her tomorrow after work," but he

137

didn't really say much to this and was just like, "Maybe another time," and then, "We'll do something at the weekend," and I said, "Sure."

We tried Bradby who of course was a long shot, and actually didn't pick up at all. Then Graz did answer but was unexpectedly unenthusiastic about the idea, just as much as Neale, saying it was, "A bit late," and that he was watching the football anyway but was up for doing something at the weekend.

So, well to be honest there wasn't exactly a hell of a lot of people to phone, even though we did try Alex and Paul afterwards (no response) and then Duncan was up for phoning Ambra for some reason 'cause he said she had some, "Cool mates," or something.

It was after the first three phone calls though that we were both pretty much looking at each other with all the energy of our plan totally drained.

I remember like… yeah as I think of myself there now I can feel again how much I totally wanted to just go out again and have a big night, like on the night I'd met Holly only a few days before and how I was so up for it and in the mood and that.

But after Ambra said she was, "Busy," and, "Sorry," I didn't even bother talking about who else there was to phone, and neither did Duncan. There was no point.

Duncan changed the CD to some Long Life Mild before going back to the armchair and sparking up the new joint. He said to me, "We could always go to a few pubs in Bracksea," and I said, "What about Firkinton though?" and that I hadn't been there in ages but he was like, "I can't really see how it's gonna happen."

To Be a Saint started up, which is a well long and chilled out song that goes on for about ten minutes, and I poured myself another drink and took a sip; still harsh but getting better.

I said, "Are we gonna finish the bottle first?" saying about how it might be fun to be, "Completely wasted before we go out," although I then thought about how it was a Tuesday and *what the hell are we gonna do?* But then changed my mind again and reckoned to myself that it might be cool anyway to at least give some random night a chance.

Duncan passed me the joint and pointed towards the *Argus* which was still lying on the sofa next to me and asked, "Can I have a look?" and I reached over and passed it to him, taking the *NME* for myself. Half laying down I opened it up and the words were all a bit of a mess. I knew then that I was more pissed than I'd thought I was.

I closed it again and looked over to Duncan who was already on the job section, quietly reading away.

The cat was staring at me again as I took a drag of the joint, which was suddenly making my head feel like a fucking pin ball machine... spinning and that... And my stomach was rumbling and moving around, like a tumble drier or something, just like my head, or maybe one of those water fountain things with wheels which are all synchronised to go on forever as long as the water keeps moving.

I got up again, steadying myself and walked over to Duncan to give him the joint back. He took it, still reading, and then I kinda half ran half walked quickly to the bathroom.

THIRTY-SEVEN

There was a piece of sick still on the tap and I wiped it off, staring at the distorted reflection of myself leaning forward, all nose and eyes and hair all over the place.

I turned to the mirror and my nose looked smaller again but my eyes were still big, and red. And my cheeks were bright red too.

I said, "I reckon I looked cooler in the tap," and laughed.

I got myself properly to my feet, feeling a bit drained of energy, but also relieved to be rid of the contents of my stomach; or at least to be rid of the uncomfortable-ness anyway.

I'd made myself sick. At first it'd just been retching but it was pretty frustrating waiting for something to come up so I'd stuck my middle finger into my throat and wiggled it around my tonsils to force myself to chuck, which I'd done five or six times in all. And on the last time the fizzing sound had started again – I'd decided to ignore it.

There was some toothpaste on the shelf. I took it and squeezed a decent amount into my mouth, swirled it around with water, gargled, spat it out, then washed my face and hands properly with soap and hot water.

I dried myself off, rolled a fag, lit it, left the bathroom and headed back to the front room to see Duncan; wondering how long I'd been in there and if he was gonna know I'd been being sick and that. But Duncan was slumped in the chair asleep, the *Argus* on the floor in front of him (so yeah, never did find out exactly how long I'd been in the bathroom).

His hair had fallen forward to almost completely cover his face and for a moment I remember he looked a bit like Colin – Colin just before he died that is; in his last few weeks I mean. Just the way he was slumped in the chair and all.

I walked over to him to check he was breathing (yeah, bit strange but I actually did this) and he was. So I took the *Argus* off the floor and went over to the couch to get my *NME*.

The fizzing sound was still there. I looked up at the cat but it was sleeping and ignoring me.

I put the *NME* where the *Argus* had been, tucked the *Argus* under my arm and then, dunno why but I gave the flat a quick once-over, looking for anything else that might've been worth taking, my eyes resting on Duncan's bag of weed and I half considered nicking some but didn't 'cause it felt a bit wrong. But, like as my hand was on the door handle I remembered the rum and went back for it – for some reason I didn't think Duncan would've minded me taking that. I mean, it tasted like shit and all and Duncan wasn't exactly a drinker (although later, the next time I saw him he was a bit pissed off about this actually).

But anyway, there I was, bottle of rum wrapped in the job supplement under my arm, cigarette in my hand, fizzing sound in my head, leaving Duncan's flat, refreshed, sober again and like, not yet ready to give up on my potential night of randomness.

I switched the light off on my way out, clicked the door behind me and then I was out into the darkness.

THIRTY-EIGHT

It was just gone nine o'clock as I dragged on my cigarette, moving the rum to my left hand and then after another drag I opened the bottle to take a swig, which tasted like shit but the fizzing sound was becoming duller and I reckon it was 'cause of the rum: pretty soon I felt it'd be gone.

It was dark of course. Almost ten o'clock I remember as I was making my way into town with no particular plan of what there was to do once I got there. I mean, I had a feeling there was always the chance I'd bump into someone I knew but even so it was a small possibility and I wasn't bargaining on it.

But, well actually I'm not completely sure if this makes sense but anyway I just had a feeling that walking into town was gonna be cool and if nothing happened when I got there then maybe I'd make it happen. And if I couldn't then trying and looking for adventure would be fun in itself – like when you're a kid and you go on a search to find a porno mag and it doesn't matter if you don't actually find one, 'cause the search is fun in itself.

So anyway, I was almost at the first bus stop in town and thinking that it might be cool to go into The Bowman for a drink when I realised I had hardly any money on me so I headed to the cash point opposite. Thinking about it now I reckon I noticed the cash point and it was this that made me remember I was short of cash. But anyway at the cash point it asked me to choose how much I wanted and instead of typing in *ten* I accidentally pressed an extra zero, ending up with getting a hundred quid out and suddenly, standing there with all these notes in my hand, I was feeling pretty excited about all the possibilities that the notes had now presented me with.

Next thing I was in the offie nearby buying a new lighter, some more backy, and some crisps and chocolate – I got an Aero, a Lion bar and a Fry's Chocolate Cream 'cause I couldn't decide on which – and I was walking around singing to myself, really having a good look around, checking all the things I could buy. Just stuff like the magazines, the different kinds of sweets and crisps (yeah there were shit loads of sweets but I just wasn't in the mood; it wasn't as it would've been if I was a kid). There was random stuff too like board games, maps and a few CDs with these natural sounds like whale music and bird songs that I found in the corner.

The fat lady behind the counter was new and took ages. I could tell she was looking at me nervously as though she was scared or something as I handed over my money and I remember wondering like, *why*, but, *whatever*, and then thinking, "Why the hell work in an off license then?"

*

On the way out I spotted Alex and Paul on the other side of the street, walking along looking bored. I remember my heart jumped when I saw them. It was like, "Fucking hell!"

When I caught up to them they asked me what I was up to and I said, all enthusiastically I suppose, "Nothing, just looking for some mates," before asking what they were up to, with them saying, "Nothing," and after a bit of silence Paul replying that they were, "Just walking around town."

I didn't really ask to join them, I just sort of did. Like I didn't really stop and chat, I simply tagged along without the need to really get permission or explain myself. It was just Alex and Paul after all.

We walked to the end of the high street, turned the corner into the old high street and then we were about half way along there when Alex went and sat down on one of the benches with me and Paul following.

I opened my crisps and started eating them, thinking how cool it was that my plan of having a random night was succeeding so far. I was with Alex and Paul on a bench in the middle of Bracksea and like, *how cool is this?*

I had a bit more rum but not much, and Alex and Paul said they didn't want any so I didn't really wanna be drinking in front of them – actually when they said they didn't want any they both said it as though it was disgusting or something. Like, what the hell was I doing drinking from a bottle of rum? As if it wasn't cool or something (I didn't tell them it was Duncan's).

So we sat for a bit, Alex and Paul talking about how Bracksea wasn't like it used to be and how it'd changed into a place taken over by all the townies with their, "All right mate," talk and *Kappa* and *Adidas* gear. They talked about all the young girls who were no longer worth chatting up with their "Hi, how are you?" conversation, and even though I didn't agree with most of what they were saying it was fun at first sitting there, saying the odd thing, nodding in agreement and making sure I went, "Yeah," at the right moments.

I must admit though, and I should really say now that pretty soon, or at least after a little while, the novelty of meeting up with Alex and Paul started to wear off.

I mean, my heart had sort of leapt when I'd seen them 'cause I was still excited from the rum, the money and the potential of my night. But it was like as soon as I joined them I couldn't help but pick up on their mood which was a lot more, low beat – although maybe it wasn't just them 'cause Bracksea did feel like a ghost town: even more so in the old high street, where the lamp posts were giving off this really dim light and there was even an old newspaper moving around the floor in the slight wind that there was. Slowly unfolding itself, page by page, which reminded me of one of those things that you see in Westerns... you know, those balls of grass which blow about out there in Arizona or wherever.

So there we were, still on the bench, still slagging off Bracksea and going on and on about how shit everything was. And I did try to say that maybe we could go to The Bowman for a drink but Alex just said, "Why?" and then Paul said that he didn't have any money anyway.

I remembered about nearly phoning them up during the day then and said to Alex about it to which he replied that he'd been, "At home all day," doing nothing but that he,

"Would've probably missed the phone anyway," 'cause he'd been playing music really loud. And when I asked Paul what he'd been up to he told me he'd, "Been fishing," which sounded like a well cool thing to have been doing in the sun and I said, "Man, I should've phoned you," but he said he'd, "Left well early," and, "Didn't catch much anyway." And yeah, Alex was then off on one about how much he hated fishing and how he couldn't see the point and that.

Finally, when Alex had finished his rant, Paul asked me, "So what's up?" (or at least what'd been up) and I said about how me and Colin were interested in getting their opinion on the whole leaving college, getting a job thing and what it'd been like for them, to which they both at the same time answered, "Shit."

Alex was then, "So how is Colin these days?" and I said, "Not too good," and he was like, "Yeah, I'm not surprised," and laughed and looked over at Paul, who suddenly came out with, "I'm sure he's okay really," which confused me a bit actually, and I replied, "What makes you say that?" and he said, "At least he doesn't have to get a job," which I must admit made me laugh too; although Alex wasn't laughing any more. (Yeah, Alex and Paul both worked for themselves but took random days off and sometimes took weeks off on end – which is why their activities were so unpredictable; why they were sometimes so hard to track down).

So anyway, yeah there was this bit of chat on the bench which lasted a short while and after that, inevitably, we got up to walk around again.

I didn't talk much this time. Like join in on their conversation with, "*Yeahs*," and, "*Reallys*," as I had previously: this wasn't 'cause I was uncomfortable or anything; I just didn't wanna.

We got to the end of the old high street, passed The Bowman, around past the fish and chip shop and cut through the church, ending up again on a bench, this time in the graveyard.

And in the same way as before it was fine sitting there at first: in fact initially it was pretty cool. The graveyard had atmosphere and it was like the perfect place to be sitting, especially at night. But after a while Alex and Paul's banter kinda died and I started getting a bit restless.

Like, it was *Alex and Paul* and they were usually so fun: I remember wondering to myself what we usually got up to when I was with them but I couldn't really think of anything other than walking or driving around doing nothing in particular.

After a few more minutes of sitting there Alex came out with, "Yep, this is Bracksea," and Paul started laughing but I didn't.

And that was when I finally said what I'd been trying not to say the whole time and asked if they had any gear with them.

But they both just said, "No," and my heart kinda sank.

THIRTY-NINE

I got out the rum again and had a couple of swigs before saying, "What shall we do then?" still feeling pissed off – although to be honest I immediately felt uncomfortable after I'd said this: like, 'cause maybe it wasn't really my place to be saying something like that I suppose.

But Alex had an idea. He said, "Let's get a pack of Marlborough," and Paul said, "Yeah." And then I said, "Yeah."

Alex was then like, "Have you got any money Chambers?" which I didn't really know how to reply to. Like, I did have money and they knew it (although they didn't know how much) but I didn't really wanna say, "Yeah, that's 'cause I have to fucking work my arse off at Price-Savers," or anything like that – there again though, I thought, I'd blagged gear off them enough times so I finally said, "Fuck it," and, "Yeah, okay."

I rolled a fag for the walk, staring at all the gravestones in front of me, thinking about how cool it'd be if we saw a ghost or something. There were shit loads of stars in the sky on that night: I mean, I guess there always is but on that night as I was sat with Alex and Paul I remember looking up and the sky was covered in them. It was kinda cool (although there was no full moon or anything).

I waited a few minutes, sort of confused about if they wanted to go immediately or like later or something and they weren't moving and yeah I was wondering how long I was gonna have to wait for them to get up until Paul finally looked over and said, "Umm, we're not coming."

I said, "What, so I've gotta pay for the fags and go and get them and you two are just gonna sit here?" and they were both like, "Yeah."

I got up, looking down at Alex and Paul slumped on the bench and I started laughing. It was just funny for some reason. The way they were just sitting there not even really looking at me.

While there I was, feeling half amused, half pissed off,

saying, "Fine," and then walking off without saying anything else.

As I was leaving the graveyard I must admit I suddenly felt a bit more paranoid about the whole dominance thing of how just 'cause I was younger I was the one who had to be sent on an errand: and then I started wondering, like the thought entered my head that they might not even be there when I returned – actually I even considered just going home and not going back at all but finally I thought, "It's *Alex and Paul*, for fuck's sake," and how they weren't that bad really and what was I expecting?

On the walk to the offie I started imagining myself at Alex and Paul's age, where I'd be and what I'd be doing. How I couldn't imagine still living in Bracksea but wondering where the hell I would be... I thought about if I'd be married too, or at least have met whoever it was I was gonna marry. And also I started thinking if I'd still be smoking pot then. Like at first reckoning that I probably wouldn't, but then figuring *why the hell not?* Imagining having a porch and smoking joints outside, watching the sunset with my wife before we went to bed.

Outside the offie there was this gang of young townie girls, aged around fourteen, fifteen, I reckoned. All standing about and sitting on the pavement, dressed in typical tracksuit bottoms, hair in ponytails, loads of make-up and that.

I remember thinking, "Fucking wonderful," when I saw them. Anticipating the comments they were probably gonna come out with as I walked past and, actually yeah, deciding that I wasn't gonna take any shit – my mood a result of the way Alex and Paul had been before I suppose.

One of the girls came up to me as I approached, sort of swaying around the path as she got closer. She had dyed blonde hair and I remember her eyes had thick black eye-liner all over them which wasn't like properly symmetrical, kinda just like two badly drawn black rings around her eyes. As though she'd put it on for the first time ever that day and had no idea how to really, apply it or whatever.

She said something to me which I didn't really understand

and I started taking the piss out of her for being obviously drunk, saying, "Aren't you a bit young to be pissed?" and then, "You nick your mum's wine again?" and she just sort of looked at me, a bit surprised and taken aback I guess, and said nothing.

Then one of the other girls came up and asked me if I'd, "Get some fags," for them and I said, "No," and that she shouldn't smoke and that smoking was bad for her health (I didn't really care, I just felt like pissing her off).

And then, as I walked past the whole group one of them shouted, "All right mate?" and I said, "Shouldn't you be in bed love?" and one of the others shouted something about *if I was offering* or something, which I didn't quite catch; but I ignored this one anyway.

Back in the offie it was the same fat lady behind the counter, giving more a look of disapproval this time as she served me (I'd just gone straight up to her; there was no need to walk around the shop or anything this time).

When I said I wanted, "Twenty Marlborough please," she asked me if they were for me and I didn't really get what she meant at first and I said, "Sort of."

And then for a moment I thought maybe she wanted some conversation so I said, "My friends are up at the graveyard and they sent me to get them," and smiled, saying, "Been sent on an errand." But she was just staring as though there was something wrong with me or something and saying nothing back.

And that was when I realised she thought I was buying the cigarettes for the girls so on the way out I gave them all a fag each, making sure the lady saw me, just to piss her off.

As I handed them out the girls were all really grateful. All like, "Thanks mate."

*

When I got back to the graveyard Alex and Paul were still there surprisingly. They both didn't seem to have moved.

I walked up to them showing them the Marlborough and

149

said about how I'd had to give some away but Alex just said, "Cool," and took one of the fags out the packet, asking Paul if he'd, "Got a light."

I stood rather than sat, accepting a Marlborough from Alex and gazed up at the church windows reflecting in the beam from the streetlamps, which looked kinda beautiful as I remember.

Smoking in the dark with the gravestones and the church behind me and Alex and Paul in front: it was sort of a cool feeling. I remember blowing the smoke out and watching it float up through the air, taking its time to disappear. And then I was blowing smoke rings and Alex noticed and, yeah rather than say anything he just started blowing smoke rings too, which were like perfect (Paul's were just like mine: not much to look at really).

So we sat on the bench and smoked through the rest of the packet, listening to a bad quality John Lipton tape on Alex's turned up walkman. And we passed around the rum too, which they wanted this time.

Alex and Paul talked to me for a bit about Glastonbury and about this old couple they'd met there who were really cool and still did drugs and that; who sounded pretty chilled out and I thought again about if I'd still smoke pot when I was older, this time imagining not only the porch but going to places like Glastonbury with my wife and kids.

When I asked Alex and Paul what bands they'd seen both of them laughed, saying they hadn't seen any and how it wasn't really, "What Glastonbury's about," and then proceeded to tell me about some of the "Funny shit," they'd got up to. Like how Paul had got this really dodgy acid which had made him think the girls camping next to them were actually witches (he was still convinced they had been). How on one of the days they'd been so fucked and had spent like hours lying in the chill out tent staring up at the roof.

After listening to them going on for a bit I said it'd be, "Cool to see Lipton there if he ever went," and they both agreed. Although Alex said that, "It'd be way better to see Lipton back in the day," like when he was good, saying how when it came to the present day Lipton he, "Probably wouldn't bother going at all."

Then Paul and Alex proceeded to argue about Lipton for a bit; I didn't really get involved. I was just staring at the graves again I think… yeah and this was when I noticed the fizzing sound had disappeared and couldn't for the life of me remember exactly when it'd stopped. (At that point? A few minutes before? Ages before? God knows).

It'd gone quiet for a few minutes when Alex asked me about how my summer had been so far, making me feel a bit uncomfortable actually, the way he was staring at me waiting for my answer.

I wondered whether he wanted some quick remark, like, "Shit," or, "Cool," or if he actually wanted me to go into some amusing story or something.

Finally though I just told the truth and said how so far there'd been a couple of good nights but some parts of it'd been, "Pretty boring," and like, "Not what I was expecting." How I'd imagined every day lazing around in the sun with my mates, drinking in the evenings and swimming in the sea but that somehow it hadn't quite worked out like this. I said about how everyone was working now too and how it was well shit.

Neither of them had much to say to this though so after a pause I decided to tell them about Holly instead.

I didn't really go into too much detail about, like my feelings, but instead just said how I thought maybe I was gonna get a girlfriend but that I'd been pretty relieved when it hadn't worked out.

But I did tell them all about the night I'd spent with her, which I thought they'd enjoy hearing about, 'cause yeah, Alex was going into details enough times with his conquests and I thought Alex at least would enjoy hearing about Holly. But neither of them really commented at all actually and to be honest I felt a bit embarrassed when I'd finished telling them about it.

I started getting this picture in my mind of Holly lying next to me on her bed. All innocent and trusting and that… and I

151

remember kinda feeling as though I'd let her down...

Paul interrupted my thoughts then, suddenly saying, "You shouldn't worry about Holly," and that she, "Wasn't important," and I... yeah that confused the hell out of me when he said this. And it was a moment before I replied with a sarcastic, "What *is*?"

But Alex then said, "I think you should know by now young man what's important and what's not," and... yeah that confused the hell out of me too and I really didn't know what to say then.

Like, I have this strong recollection of looking up with them both staring at me and the graveyard and the stars and the church were all behind them and stuff and it all, like everything, was feeling a bit weird all of a sudden. Like, I dunno, half of me wanted to laugh, half of me was insulted and half was like... it felt as though they knew something I didn't and it was sort of making me well uncomfortable.

I thought for a moment about how to reply, trying to think of a clever and maybe humorous response, but then before I knew it I'd said, "Do you mean Colin?" and Alex was dragging on his cigarette saying, "What do *you* think?"

FORTY

What actually happened and what I remember happening to me are different things. I guess I should say this now; just in case I haven't made it clear before or anything. Like, I'm pretty sure that when I passed out the first time, when I was with Charlotte, it was 'cause I was tired or 'cause of the drink or something. But I'm still not sure about the second time when I was with Holly. (Like, was there a big guy then? Did I actually pass out at all?)

As with this incident, I can clearly remember what Alex and Paul were talking about and some of the things they were coming out with, but that's not to say it's exactly what went on... Although it might be; who knows?

But anyway, I asked Alex after a few more drags on my current Marlborough what he was talking about and he said, "Why do you think we're here Chambers?" and I remember I wasn't exactly sure what he was talking about. And the way he was looking at me it was like the way my mum used to before my dad had left, all those years before; when she still gave a shit and that: Alex's expression really did have this sudden maternal, kinda patronising thing going on about it... It was even similar to when Charlotte had been asking me about Colin a few weeks earlier (or however long it'd been); at least I was feeling the same way: tripped out and that; but at the same time wanting to stay in the moment.

I said, after thinking for a bit, "'Cause I want you to be I suppose."

And then Alex and Paul together said, "But why do you want us to be here?" and I said, "'Cause I wanna have a random night," and they both laughed.

Then Paul said, "So why are we in the graveyard?" and I was like, "'Cause it's cool here," and they laughed again, and... I think by then I was maybe eighty percent sure that they were messing with my head but I was still feeling a bit weirded out.

And yeah, I was thinking about how I could continue talking in a way that'd appear to them as if I knew that they were messing with me but also, just in case... well, there was stuff I wanted to ask them all of a sudden.

I said to Paul, "Why don't you think Holly's important?" but he didn't answer me.

Then Alex said, "Have another drink Chambers," and held out the bottle of rum towards me and I took it and had a swig, racking my brain over how I should use this sudden opportunity to talk or whatever before out of nowhere I came out with, "So why do I feel so guilty about Colin then?" and Alex, immediately and sort of aggressively said, "You were there man, you were with him, 'course you're gonna feel that way!"

Then Paul was saying about how if anything ever happened to Alex he'd, "Probably lose it too," and Alex started laughing, calling Paul a, "Fucking stoner," and then they were off again into one of their banters, leaving me to my thoughts over what the hell, "Lose it too," was supposed to mean and whether to take them seriously and stuff.

*

To be perfectly honest I'm pretty sure that the following definitely happened in a dream. Although there again I'm not completely certain about this so I'm just gonna say that even though it most likely happened in my head after I'd passed out, I'm gonna tell this as though it actually took place.

So what went on was... well suddenly I had this really strange feeling that I'd sat there on that bench with Alex and Paul before: kinda like déjà vu. And my head was spinning and I was starting to feel faint but there was something else I really wanted to ask them. Like... something I'd forgotten; something important.

I couldn't for the life of me imagine what this all-so-important question was though. And I know definitely that the thing I did manage to ask just before I passed out wasn't the thing I'd been trying to remember... although... well, I dunno. This is all a bit confusing actually.

But anyway, I looked over to Alex and Paul as they were

talking and interrupted them by shouting, "HEY!" and they both like shut up for an instant, but after that started laughing, as though what I'd said was really funny or something... and yeah, then they were just carrying on with their banter and ignoring me again.

But I wasn't giving up and I shouted, "HEY!" once more and they both stopped and turned their heads to face me. And that was when I asked, "Are we really here?" for some reason.

Alex was like, "What?" and I repeated myself with, "Like here, in the graveyard, in Bracksea. Are we really here?"

I could see Paul looking at Alex with this totally bemused expression, while Alex was just staring at me, all concerned and that, finally coming out with a, "Hey man, are you okay?" and Paul was then like, "Yeah man, you all right?"

And the last thing I remember is managing to say, "Yeah," to both of them before everything disappeared.

FORTY-ONE

The story of the final day when Colin was alive is... well, it's something I haven't really wanted to go into for a lot of reasons. Mainly 'cause the whole situation with mine and Colin's final real conversation is a memory I've consciously been trying to avoid thinking about for so long and, for the most part, what ended up kinda happening was that it seemed to get stuck there, right in the back of my head; which is where it's stayed for even more than a hell of a long time. (But yeah, admittedly to not talk about this day would be wrong: I know this for sure now).

So the last day when I actually saw Colin was a Friday. And as far as Fridays go it was a shit one, right from the start.

When I woke up it was raining; the pelting of raindrops against my window never being the greatest sound to hear in the morning. And then when I went downstairs my mum was still in, which I'd totally not been expecting, and she was all half in the front room half in the kitchen, tidying up the house for some reason, still in her dressing gown, telling me that she'd called in sick for her job and was gonna be home all day and, "Make the most of this opportunity," to give the house a, "Spring clean," – which she randomly did at times; like when the state of the place was getting really bad.

So I took my tea and toast back up to my room and had breakfast in there, listening to a bit of daytime Radio One shite, and then when I couldn't put up with any more of that I put on a Hessian CD and had a couple of fags out my window, waiting for three o'clock to come round; or at least to draw closer.

And when my mum came into my room to shout at me about how messy it was and like how I had to, "Tidy this shit up," before going to work I remember thinking, *fucking typical*. Just 'cause, well bad days are like that, aren't they? It's never just one thing.

To be honest as I sat there on the floor in the middle of all these piles of clothes, CDs, college folders and books and

156

crap that I was slowly putting into order, all I really wanted to do was just get back into bed and wait for the next day to come around.

*

As soon as I got in to work The Terminator was all on my and everyone else's back about some visit we were getting from this guy from head office who was like *Mr Price-Savers*. He'd apparently been supposed to be coming in the morning but hadn't arrived yet and everyone, like the whole store was still on panic stations, totally freaking out.

I'd gotten out the back about five, ten minutes late ('cause of the fucking bus) and everybody was stacking down a new set of boards that'd just come in from another store and it was all loading up L-shapes with The Terminator giving me a sarcastic, "Nice of you to turn up Chambers," and pushing one of them towards me.

So there we were, me, Bradby and Neale, working our arses off non-stop for the next couple of hours, the Mr Price-Saver's guy still not appearing. All the managers getting increasingly agitated, us totally pissed off about having no break – and then when we'd gone through all the stock The Terminator gave us the task of cleaning the whole fucking department which we were doing up until around six o'clock or whatever time it was when Hitler decided that the guy wasn't gonna turn up and it'd all been for nothing.

What made matters worse though was that just as the three of us were walking to the canteen, like when it'd all calmed down and most of the managers had pissed off home, I got collared by Vader and told to go help out the deli, which I'd only ever worked on once before and wasn't properly trained on. And I tried to say this to Vader but he wasn't having any of it, all like, "Get over there now!" while Neale and Bradby were already disappearing round the corner, chatting away, no real qualms about "*man down!*" and that.

I was stuck on the deli for ages too, 'cause it turned out someone had called in sick and there was no one to replace me once I'd got on there (yeah it was just me and Little Miss Busy). And even though eating the range of free food in front of me was nice enough, I wasn't getting much chance to try any of it 'cause of all the early evening customers that were now piling in; I was soon rushed off my feet to say the least.

So it totally wasn't a good day for me, already. And I wasn't exactly in the best of moods when the phone on the deli rang with Little Miss Busy holding it out towards me saying, "It's for you."

FORTY-TWO

It was on the deli where I took the call from Colin; the line of customers in front of me being my kinda unwanted audience. I remember it was weird and a bit of a surprise 'cause I never really had people phoning up Price-Savers to speak to me: but there was Little Miss Busy, holding the deli phone out towards me with an irritated, sarcastic sort of expression saying, "It's for you Chambers."

I went over and took the phone off her, saying, "Hello?" into the receiver, feeling a bit pissed off, like wondering who the hell it was and if it was some sort of practical joke or something that maybe Raver-Dave or someone had decided to pull: but no, it was Colin, something I really hadn't been expecting and totally wasn't in the mood for.

The first thing he said into the phone was, "Is that Chambers?" me replying with a, "Yeah," and him saying, "It's Colin," and I said about how I knew it was 'cause of his voice and he was like, "Right."

There was then this bit of silence while I waited for him to say something more but he didn't – I could hear him breathing into the phone though so I knew he was still there – so I said, after the pause had gone on for a bit longer, "What's up?"

Colin replied with a, "How're you doing?" and I said that I was all right but work was shit and he said, "Cool."

Then, quite plain and to the point I suppose, Colin came out with, "I need to see you tonight," and about how he needed my help with something: all totally sounding... a bit desperate to be honest; in a weird sort of way: like there was no way I could refuse and that.

Yeah, it wasn't, "Do you fancy going out for a drink?" or, "You up for doing something tonight?" – No leading up to asking me to meet him.

It was just Colin saying that he needed to see me and when I asked him, "Why?" he simply replied that it was, "Important," and, "I'll tell you later," and when I said, "What is?" and, "You can tell me now," he was just like,

159

"I'll be at The Bowman from nine," and, "What time do you finish work?" and I said that I finished at nine but I'd get down there as soon as I could.

The way he was speaking was a bit weird though. Like he wasn't happy about whatever it was he had to tell me. I remember wondering like what the hell he had to be so unhappy about and it was a bit frustrating to be honest, the whole, "I'll tell you later," thing.

But yeah, I didn't get the chance to find out any more 'cause this was how the call ended, with Colin saying again that I should, "Meet me in The Bowman at nine," and I was saying, "Sure," and putting the phone down, feeling kinda half relieved half pissed off to be getting back to the waiting customers, but with no inkling as to... like not yet really as bothered as I guess I should've been with what the conversation had just been about and what I was in for.

*

There's stuff I should say here about the last few months before Colin died. Just about mine and Colin's... like our relationship I guess; if you can call it that ('cause we were both blokes after all).

Basically what I've gotta tell is that when Colin phoned me up on the deli we weren't exactly best friends any more. I mean we were still mates and hadn't really had some big falling out or anything. But we weren't as close as we had been. We'd drifted apart a bit, for certain.

Thinking about why and that, well it's difficult to pinpoint exactly when it happened so as to what the cause was I'm not completely sure. Just 'cause it's kinda something that at least *I* didn't notice until the distance between us was already there. Like when we suddenly weren't hanging out every day and had ceased to be the *Colin-and-Chambers*, entity – *never see one without the other* thing.

And yeah, like, none of this had anything to do with Tanya, 'cause that happened afterwards, which I know for definite 'cause I totally wasn't there when they met (no idea *how*

160

they got together actually) and still don't have that much of a clue as to why it all went wrong – actually it all happened pretty quickly and during this time I was busy with the whole exams thing and when I was going out it was just to Duncan's for a bit of television and weed and that.

But yeah, after the break-up Colin suddenly had different mates and I was too involved with getting through one shite test after another… and it wasn't a case of me ignoring any need I felt to be there for him 'cause he really did seem to be all right. He had his new townie friends and nothing that much had changed with us when we *were* meeting up (most of the time round Duncan's) – although I must admit too that the whole being his sidekick, follower thing had gradually been starting to piss me off a lot more of late. In many ways I was feeling happy for Colin to have found other people to hang out with. Something I feel pretty ashamed to even think about now to be honest; but it's true.

Anyway though, what I'm just gonna say is that, yeah, as to the whole psychology and reason why things weren't quite the same as they'd been before… there's nothing that I can really talk about with anything other than speculation.

I guess it's simply a case of the only thing that I'm really able to say with any certainty is that, ultimately, what'd been a problem I thought we'd solve eventually turned out to be something I never got the chance to put right.

*

After the phone call with Colin I had to go back to serving customers again straight away. The queue had been building up the whole time and now there were like ten people or something, tickets in their hands, all waiting for my attention.

Little Miss Busy did ask me, "Who was that?" sort of a bit pissed off and sarcastic, 'cause I reckon she knew or had the idea it was one of my friends arranging to go out or whatever. And yeah I was gonna make up some story to explain this important reason for having been called up, like

161

'cause of a grandmother dying or that my mum was sick: but then I thought, "Fuck it," and admitted it'd been one of my mates, saying, "Soz," and, "It won't happen again."

So after that I was just serving and slicing ham, cutting up cheese and bits of pork pie, handing out scotch eggs and shit. And although I was starting to get a bit apprehensive about meeting up with Colin later (just 'cause of the way he'd been on the phone and all) I didn't really have time to think about it too much until finally I got to go for a break.

I remember sitting in the canteen wondering what the hell was up, imagining what Colin was gonna say: figuring how maybe it was gonna be something to do with him going away actually. Just 'cause, I dunno, I reckoned it was the only bad news that Colin could possibly have to tell me – yeah, I'd decided, just from his tone of voice, like his seriousness when talking to me that whatever this important thing was… well my reasoning was that it was more likely to be bad news than good. Especially with the day I was having as well, like, I dunno; it just felt like that if you know what I mean.

And yeah, the only other thing I could imagine was that Colin was for some reason gonna say to me about how he wanted to go back to being best mates again – but this was unlikely I figured: and a bit weird too. So even though I did consider this possibility (like, my imagination working overtime as Colin was telling me all about how his townie mates were all wankers, begging me to take him back) I dismissed the idea as being doubtful to say the least.

Sereme was with me at the time, sitting opposite me as I was thinking about all of this, like miles away and not really talking to her. She was eating this chocolate cream cake as I remember now. Totally enjoying the hell out of it, eating it slowly, and kinda sexily I started to notice after a while, and I made a joke about if she wanted me to, "Leave you two alone," and she laughed.

But that was it really as far as talking to Sereme went. Although I think she also asked me if I was, "Up to anything tonight?" and I replied I was just going down The Bowman for a couple of pints and she said, "Cool."

I walked into the smoking room by myself and rolled a cigarette, soon reading the paper that was in there, trying not to think too much about Colin anymore 'cause the whole thing was starting to piss me off a bit. Like, I remember just wishing my evening had been free and was feeling that not only did I have to deal with getting through my shift but now there was the added task of getting down The Bowman as soon as I could and having some sort of serious conversation with someone who I really wasn't that much in the mood to meet.

I mean, if later I'd just decided to head down The Bowman as a spur of the moment thing and met Colin there by accident then maybe I'd have been in a better mood. But I wasn't really feeling the energy with the whole having my evening already planned for me, if you know what I'm saying.

So I was reading the paper but the words were all a blur and it was hard to concentrate 'cause I was tired and the cigarette was making my mouth taste like crap – probably something to do with the fact I hadn't eaten properly; I'd only had a coffee and chocolate bar before and that'd been the first thing since breakfast.

And yeah, before long I was starting to feel pretty depressed actually; maybe the lack of food as I say. Or could even have been something to do with the fact nobody else was in there with me. Just my reflection in the window to keep me company whilst outside the sun had already disappeared. Dusk was hitting in, while the rain was still pouring down, totally miserable and grey.

While there I was, trying to cheer myself up with the thought that soon it'd be summer and I'd be free and was gonna get the hell out of Price-Savers, spend each day doing whatever the hell I wanted to do… and how it was all gonna be so fucking great.

FORTY-THREE

I got out of work late. There'd been a queue of customers at the deli and Little Miss Busy had gone home by then and the guy I was then working with had gone for a break at like half eight but hadn't come back till ten past. And to make matters worse the last customer I was finishing up with was this lady who was wanting Parma ham cut extra thin and I was making a right mess of it 'cause of it being well difficult to slice and she kept making me do it again, not satisfied with any of the pieces I was giving her.

So I missed the nine-twenty bus and the next one was at ten-twenty and I was pretty pissed off and not really knowing what to do. Almost kicking the bus shelter in frustration actually, before rolling a cigarette to calm down, wondering whether to get a taxi, head over to the train station or even to just walk; which took forty minutes but I was feeling that at least it'd be giving me something to be getting on with.

It wasn't raining any more. The night had that weird feeling when you can tell it's just been raining. Something to do with the atmospheric pressure; I dunno. Like the air was all fresh and everything was noticeably still.

I looked around me wondering what to do, gazing up and noticing how there was a full moon (which I remember thinking was kinda cool) and then over into the distance towards the direction in which the bus would be coming from in an hour or so, watching all the car lights emerge from the coast road, listening to the hush of the spaced out traffic…

And this was when suddenly I spotted the bus from far away, knowing it was my bus immediately 'cause the lights were higher than those of all the other cars; although sometimes you do get ghost buses at around that time of night – I call them this anyway; basically I mean buses with no passengers and the sign turned off – driving around for fuck knows what purpose.

But no, it wasn't a ghost bus. It was the real one. Which I

164

figured must've been delayed or something; yeah it made a change to be happy about a bus being late for once.

And I guess I *was* pretty happy for a moment. At least I remember shouting, "Fucking result!" to myself, before dragging on the last remains of my fag.

I checked my pockets for the fifty pence needed to get me back home into Bracksea, the bus coming round the corner already, stopping in front of me with a squeal of the breaks and a, *whoosh* from whatever it is that makes that sound when a bus comes to a halt.

As the doors opened some people were getting off, which, if you really wanna know was a couple of girls who looked like they'd been out in Firkinton (shopping or whatever, carrying bags and stuff), a man in a suit obviously returning from work (fuck that!) and a woman with a little kid who was crying about something; although I couldn't tell what.

I got on, paying my money to the bus guy and then headed upstairs, immediately regretting my choice 'cause there was this bunch of townie lads and slags up there, all shouting to each other, being really lairy and that.

They were taking the piss out of this old man too, who was dressed in an old fashioned suit and a hat, saying all this stuff that I was trying my best not to tune in to. While he was just sitting there not saying anything back and kinda staring into space, obviously desperate for the bus to hurry up and reach his stop.

I remember wishing I had my walkman with me as I sat there at the front, watching the trees fly by on either side; then concentrating on the cats-eyes whizzing by under the bus, speeding us along the road to Bracksea and whatever lay in store for me when I got there.

*

The first thing I thought about when I got in The Bowman was how I wanted to get pissed. Not totally wasted or anything. But I needed a pint or two to get rid of the trapped feeling of being stuck at work and on the deli for the last however many hours it'd been.

It was a Friday night and there were loads of people in there, everyone drunk and shouting and having a good time. It felt pretty good to finally be somewhere I could just get some alcohol in me and relax: I think this is why I made headway to get a pint in rather than look around for Colin first; 'cause I was mostly interested in taking that first sip of a new pint; what with the long day I'd had at work and all.

So I immersed myself in the crowd at the bar, pushing my way to the front, trying to catch Ambra's attention once I was there, although not having much luck 'cause I was surrounded by tonnes of other people also fighting to get served.

Finally I caught the notice of one of the other staff – yeah it was the owner who was suddenly standing in front of me; this middle-aged guy with a shiny balding head – and I said I wanted, "Two pints of Fosters and a packet of dry roasted peanuts."

I remember him asking me if I was, "Having a good night?" as he poured my drink and I was saying about how it was only my first pint and, "Maybe when I get pissed it will be," which made him laugh. And this confused me at first actually. Like the way he was finding what I said funny 'cause I was being serious and didn't mean it as a joke: and then I was thinking about how he was a bar owner and he should've understood what I meant.

Anyway, I stood there waiting for my order, half looking at Ambra, wondering if she'd come over to talk to me, thinking about what I'd say if she did. She was wearing these short jeans and a tight T-shirt with this pattern involving circles of reds, blues, yellows and greens, which was well fun to stare at 'cause the longer I watched for, the more it seemed as though the circles were moving; which was a quite cool effect.

But she didn't catch me staring, even when I'd got my pint and was really feeling like having a chat before seeing Colin; wherever the fuck he was.

Thinking about it now I suppose I really *should've* been

picking up my pint and leaving the bar to go and search for him.

At that moment though, what with having just finished a shit day at work, I wasn't really feeling a hell of a lot of motivation to do anything other than stay where I was, sipping my pint, finishing off my dry roasted peanuts: just 'cause I wanted to have a few minutes to myself I guess. To relax and that: wind down.

But when finally I felt a hand on my shoulder and Colin was standing there saying, "What the fuck are you doing Chambers?" and, "Didn't you see me when you got in?" I suddenly felt, I dunno, *stunned* almost... like this bolt of electricity had hit me out of nowhere.

And yeah, for a minute I really did start to wonder what the fuck I *was* doing.

FORTY-FOUR

There was nowhere for us to sit according to Colin. I mean, I was happy enough to stay at the bar but I knew it wasn't the best place for a proper talk, or at least for anything other than shouting the odd pointless comment to each other, which I knew already wasn't gonna be the sort of thing me and Colin were likely to be doing.

So I didn't argue or like come out with anything to contrast Colin's suggestion that we should, "Take our pints outside," and talk there.

I followed Colin though the crowd and then we were pushing ourselves through the doors and out into the beer garden, Colin choosing the big round table right in the middle of the area to sit down on; one of those wooden picnic set ups with a circular bench seat attached that you have to lift your legs over.

The night was again noticeably fresh as soon as we got out there. And I actually have this strong recollection of taking a deep breath and letting out a big sigh before I was then looking over at the moon and the stars above the garden's wall; and then my eyes were resting on the rooftops and I was thinking about how I never usually noticed or saw rooftops when walking around Bracksea... but there they were.

And then Colin was interrupting my thoughts on all this by asking, as he had done on the phone earlier that day, "What's up?" and, "How's it all going?" and I said, "Shit day at work but it's nice to be out now," and added, "Could do with getting a bit more pissed though."

Rather than reply to me or anything like that Colin simply took out some of his backy and started rolling up a cigarette for himself. And then he was looking at the windows of the pub behind us, watching all the people in there as they were carrying on with their usual Friday night antics.

I started rolling a fag too, although this time rather than search around for something to stare at I was just looking at Colin, noticing for the first time how thin he'd seemed to have gotten since the last time I'd properly registered his, I dunno, like, physique, build, or whatever. But there he was: long hair over his face covering this kinda gaunt appearance; looking a bit like Duncan actually; of all people.

And yeah I wanted to say to him then, "You don't look too good," or something like this, but I didn't. Instead I just drew on my cigarette, waiting and like wondering what he was gonna come out with.

He was just sitting there though, saying nothing, staring behind me through the window of the pub still.

What Colin was wearing was the same as me: jeans, a T-shirt, and a hoody that'd before been tied round his waist was now on top of the table next to my Patterson hoody; which I'd done the same with. Our T-shirts were of the same V-neck style; although his was white with blue writing on and mine was black with red writing on.

I remember feeling that it was a bit strange actually; or at least interesting. Like how we were wearing similar clothes and all: and then my mind started going off on one about how maybe it was 'cause we'd been mates for a long time and there was most likely gonna be loads of stuff we probably had and always would have in common for the rest of our lives. Just 'cause of how little parts of our personalities had probably like, brushed off on each other – and I was almost starting a conversation about this too; but I didn't.

Instead I said, "So what's going on then?" and Colin was like, "What?" and I repeated myself, using the different words of, "What's this big thing you wanna tell me?"

And I reckon then that maybe Colin could tell what I was thinking, or at least what I *had* been thinking for most of the day, ever since the phone call, 'cause he replied with a, "You don't wanna hear about it," which totally took me by surprise actually.

Just 'cause, like I knew immediately what he meant by this and how he understood my lack of interest, realising how of course it must've been obvious to him the whole while; and maybe that's why he'd taken his time to say something to me

169

and had just been sitting there silently.

But I didn't give anything away as to how I knew what he was talking about. Instead I came out with, "I dunno what you mean," and he was like, "You're not in the mood to listen to me talking about my bullshit problems," and again described how I didn't wanna hear about it.

So of course I then said that I did.

FORTY-FIVE

There're a couple of dreams I used to get quite often around that time... during that summer I mean, after Colin had died. And yeah, to tell the truth I still have them now on the odd occasion; usually when I've eaten too much cheese.

The first one involves college and starts off during an exam. There're little details which aren't always the same of course, but basically it goes something like this:

Firstly I'm sitting there in an exam room looking at this problem on a test paper.

I dunno what test or subject it is. I just know it's pissing me off 'cause I can't quite manage to get it right, make it work or whatever. Like, it's probably maths or something: some problem I'm calculating again and again but never getting the answer I need... Or it could be biology I suppose, with me trying to think about what exactly I'm supposed to be writing; or maybe English and I'm having trouble with the words and expressing myself and all.

But anyway, yeah it's doing my head in and pissing me off and then I'm suddenly up and walking out of there, heading towards the door and I can't see what's around me but I know there're other people looking at me; although I don't care: like I'm not particularly bothered or anything.

Next I'm floating down this empty corridor on my way to the common room, and then suddenly I'm in the common room looking around to see where Colin is.

Everyone seems to have gone though, the place is pretty much empty, apart from a pack of guys by the pool table whose faces I can't or don't look at. Although I know they're the lads who're usually hanging around in that spot 'cause there's nothing weird about them being there or anything.

But yeah, there's no sign of Colin anywhere.

And I'm about to turn to leave, thinking I should probably try somewhere else when this girl with red hair called Julie – who I understand in the dream to be one of Neale's friends – is all of a sudden standing there in front of me, shouting out at me, "Are you looking for Neale?" and I tell her I'm not and that I'm looking for Colin.

She gives me this blank expression when I say this... and then as she stands there looking at me she suddenly opens up her lips really wide and smoke starts coming from the inside of her mouth, loads of it, which is quickly beginning to fill the room almost – and weirdly I feel half turned on by this actually; or at least I'm finding her to be well sexy despite it all.

But anyway I'm then telling her that actually I *am* looking for Neale and as soon as I say this she closes her mouth and the smoke disappears and she's smiling at me, which is a nice sweet smile, and saying to me, "You're Colin aren't you?" and for some reason I'm then replying that I am and how I'm sorry for trying to mislead her; or something like this, and she's answering, "Don't worry about it," and about how, "It could happen to anyone," which I don't quite understand. Although I don't get the chance to ask her anything more 'cause before I can she's telling me that Neale's, "Out by the picnic benches," and apparently he's looking for me 'cause he's got things he wants to say to me.

So then I'm floating down the corridor again on my way to the picnic tables, feeling kinda hungry as I start to think about picnics... and before I know it I'm sitting there with Neale, Graz, Colin and Bradby and it's a nice sunny day and we're all sharing a joint and talking about this Julie girl, how much of a cow she is. And I've no idea as to why everyone's so angry with her or anything; just that I'm pissed off with her too for whatever the reason is.

And as we're all deep into this like bitchy conversation I remember about how Neale has something he wants to tell me... except it's not Neale it's Colin who I ask 'cause suddenly the person who has something to tell me has changed from Neale to Colin and yeah, I'm asking Colin what it is he wanted me to know about.

And typically of dreams, this is where it all ends.

*

172

In the second dream – again something I actually still experience now from time to time – I'm sitting on one of the picnic tables outside The Bowman with Colin, just like I did on the last night when I saw him alive.

Except in the dream it's not just Colin who's there 'cause after a while I notice that Tanya – the girl who Colin was seeing for that short time just before he died – is there with him and they're both talking to me and it's like they're telling me some sort of bad news and being all sympathetic and a little patronising actually, just the way they're all so *together* and looking at me like I'm some sort of kid or something.

Colin's wearing his Leaters jacket and has his hair tied back in a pony tail, while Tanya's just looking like Tanya; nothing noticeably strange about her or anything

So I'm listening to them both as they go on at me, and although I can't really say here what they're telling me – like their words or anything 'cause it's not the sort of dream where I can hear sounds – I know it's got something to do with the fact that Colin is leaving.

Yeah, it's not that *they* are leaving, which is a bit strange, 'cause, I dunno, like the way they're seeming so like a couple you'd think that she'd be going with him in this dream. But no, it's that Colin's leaving, not Tanya.

Anyway, so the whole time I can feel they're persuading me, or like pleading with me to accept this but I'm not really that interested, or at least they're continuing to be like not satisfied with whatever expression I'm giving them. And then I'm looking over at the rooftops of the houses behind The Bowman to see that they're all completely covered in seagulls, which at first seem to be sleeping, but then I'm suddenly realising that they're dead: like all of them.

Then suddenly on the picnic table and on the floor all around us are cats which are all sleeping and not dead. When I notice them I find I'm totally well angry at the cats 'cause, I dunno, probably something to do with the fact that they're cats and 'cause of how cats kill birds.

And this is how this dream ends: with me being completely

173

pissed off with all the cats, which are then getting up and skulking around, looking all satisfied with themselves; arrogant, as cats often do.

When I look up at Colin and Tanya to ask them about what's going on they're no longer there. And I'm just sitting there alone with all these cats.

FORTY-SIX

The only proper time I really met Tanya was round Duncan's flat on one evening when I'd been up late studying for this maths exam that I had the next morning and I felt like a bit of weed and television as a reward.

It was about half eleven, nearly twelve o'clock when I got round there. Duncan answered the door, saying, "All right Chambers," and that they'd just started *The Sarsaparilla* and how it was, "Good timing," and then asked if I wanted tea and I was following him straight into the kitchen to see three cups laid out with the tea bags and hot water in, Duncan getting a new mug out the cupboard, taking a teabag, pouring some water in from the kettle and was then in the fridge, swearing about how he, "Could've sworn I had some milk left," and, "Fuck's sake," and that.

I said I didn't mind powdered if he had any and he looked back answering, "Hardly the real thing though is it?" but I persuaded him not to worry about it and, "I bet they're all too stoned to notice anyway," and Duncan was saying about how when you're stoned you're more likely to notice and all that.

But yeah, anyway, I asked him then who else was in the flat and he said, "Colin and Tanya," and I was like, "Tanya?" and yeah, when I said that he looked at me a bit funny, like it was strange I didn't know who she was.

And when he said, "His new bird," I felt a bit embarrassed I remember, and came out with, "Been too fucking busy to notice I guess," (just 'cause I suppose it was weird for me to not know about something that was going on with Colin) and he was like, "Yeah, they met just over a week ago."

I then said, "So what's she like?" but he just answered, "All right I suppose," and that was it. And I did think about asking if she was fit but figured I was gonna see for myself soon enough.

So when I did walk into the front room with Duncan, carrying two mugs of tea, and saw Tanya for the first time I must admit I didn't think she was particularly fit. I mean she

175

was nice enough looking and that. But her hippy-girl image didn't really do it for me.

She had like scraggly dyed orange hair, was wearing flared jeans and a cardigan, and had black-rimed glasses.

So yeah, complete hippie-girl – although the way she took the cup from me was quite, I dunno, pretty feminine if you know what I mean; and that did sort of make her attractive for a moment in a weird sort of way.

But yeah, it was more of a cool and kinda pretty thing rather than sexy. And it was like, yeah I didn't feel jealous or anything like that: actually I felt kinda happy for Colin.

The way they were sitting together too, and like how they spoke to each other intimately as we were watching the film, I could tell he was into her.

Just 'cause of how he wasn't all treating her like his little, I dunno, fashion accessory and that: it seemed like he actually felt comfortable with her sitting there next to him.

*

So of course Tanya wasn't actually there on the night in the beer garden outside The Bowman. It was just me and Colin. Colin telling me I didn't really wanna know whatever the hell he was about to go into and me saying that I did.

And of course now's the part where you probably expect me to describe to you the whole scene of Colin saying how he was gonna kill himself later that night: something I've avoided talking about for so long that to be honest it's all but impossible to really repeat with any like clarity as to how the conversation actually went.

What I do remember though is Colin's first words of, "I don't feel like I'm really here anymore," which I totally thought was some sort of him going into one of his bullshit comments on life that I'd already got sick of listening to by then... like a typical example of those random philosophical statements he often seemed to come out with at me for all those years when I was more than happy to nod my head saying, "Yeah," and, "Totally," at all the appropriate

176

moments.

But although of course in many ways it was the perfect example of one of these, it was different this time, just 'cause, like the way he was speaking was a lot less trying to teach me something or to sound intelligent or whatever. This time it was almost as if he didn't care how I reacted.

And I suppose if he hadn't have tricked me with the whole, "You don't wanna hear about it," thing I might have reacted a lot worse than I did (to be honest I almost got up and walked away as soon as he began the whole thing) but that's not to say I didn't behave like a bit of an arsehole.

For example I remember I wasn't really looking at him as much as I knew I should've been. And when he was pointing to the people through the window behind us saying that most of them weren't, "Really here either," I remember making a sarcastic comment about how, "Yeah, I could do with another pint myself now that you mention it."

Colin didn't seem affected by my cynicism though. He just carried on talking, going on and on about how all of us were avoiding the reality of what was really going on in our minds.

Giving examples of not only how we were always getting stoned and pissed but of the pointless conversations we used to fill in the silences, of television and the films we were always, "Gawking at," round Duncan's, and our exams that we'd all been so, "Preoccupied with," and the jobs that were soon to be, "Taking over our lives."

He was even talking about girls too, saying about how dangerous they were, how he'd, "Lost myself completely," when he was with Tanya. Saying he'd no longer known what was going on in his head anymore 'cause the whole time he'd been thinking about what he should be wanting to do (to please her) and then when finally he'd got rid of her he'd felt, "Free, and able to be myself again," but that, "The terrifying thing was," it'd only lasted a short time and, "It was just a couple of days before I realised that I was no longer actually certain as to what *myself* was," and how that was when he'd realised, like, "The horror of everything

177

around us," as he was describing it; or something like this.

When he said it all I was only half listening of course, but when he got to the last part I asked him, "So what're you gonna do about it then," like not really expecting an answer or anything: kinda hoping he was gonna hurry up and come to some sort of conclusion.

At the point when I said this though he didn't reply with anything about killing himself as you might expect he would've done.

Instead he just described to me how, "Sometimes I go up to the cliffs above the golf course and sit there on the edge by myself, 'cause I want to, and need to experience what reality actually is: listen to the sound of the wind and the sea and just think *this is what I am*."

And weird as it sounds he kinda grabbed my attention for a minute when he said this.

I started imagining what it'd be like to be up there, "Alone with the elements," and whether it'd be all peaceful and stuff...

But when I said to him "Does it work?" he just kinda replied, "Sort of," and then, "Not really as much as I thought it would," and he was then looking down at his beer and saying, "Maybe it's just me, maybe there's something wrong with my head," and I was saying, "Yeah you might have a point there," and laughing but Colin wasn't laughing and then he was suddenly asking me to, "Come up there with me tonight," but I was saying that I couldn't be arsed and, "Maybe another time," 'cause I was a bit tired and wanted to be getting back home.

FORTY-SEVEN

The last time I ever saw Colin dead was during that time in the café; the time when I got myself the toasted cheese sandwich and slice of chocolate cake and we read a bit of the *NME* together.

Just before I turned around to pay was the point where I saw him last. Him telling me he was gonna, "Wait outside," for me only to find that he'd disappeared once I'd paid and got out there.

So yeah, I never actually had the chance to say to Colin what I'd been needing to ask him: mainly that is, whether it would've actually made any difference if I'd gone up to the cliffs to stop him – and of course whether he actually did jump off at all or if it was simply a case of it being some sort of unfortunate accident.

To add to this though… well there was other stuff I needed to talk about too; just stuff about what he'd said to me on that last night and that; and what he'd meant by it all.

Thinking about it now I guess I really did feel like I was gonna see him again, so this could be some explanation as to why I wasn't in any sort of hurry or anything; I dunno.

But yeah, just as when he'd died the first time his disappearance was so sudden and unexpected that I was never able to give myself any decent sort of closure.

So, feeling in need of the closure thing I suppose, what I did at the end of that summer was I wrote myself a letter, which was a bit of a crazy thing to do I know… and it's difficult to really explain as to how the hell I got the idea in my head to do it in the first place; just that I did.

Once it was written though, and read and re-read a few times I did feel better and that.

And this in many ways is where the Colin incident basically ended for me: with me folding this piece of paper up and putting it inside one of my old college folders at the bottom of a box at the back of my wardrobe in my bedroom, which is where it's stayed ever since.

*

Now this thing, as I say, I wrote myself. It's not from Colin or anything 'cause Colin never left me any goodbye note. He just left me that final conversation; although this is kinda what the letter is anyway.

What I did you see was I tried to remember and go through in my head what he'd actually said to me on that last night outside The Bowman. I wanted to try and make sense of it. The whole random speech he gave me on why he was on his way up to the cliffs in the first place.

And this is what the letter is mostly about:

CHAMBERS
For the last few months now you've probably noticed how things with me haven't been the same.

And of course this lead to a strain in our friendship that I hope to hell we manage to resolve when I meet you tonight – although if we don't you shouldn't worry about this because I want you to know now that YOU'VE ALWAYS BEEN A GOOD MATE.

And that's why tonight I'll be telling you all about what's been troubling my state of mind and pretty much driving me crazy.

Even though I know you won't be listening Chambers. I could tell this when I spoke to you on the phone today – But don't worry! I only want you to be there and if you turn up then you'll have done more than enough!

Now as I say, strange things have been going on in my head which I'll do my best to explain tonight.

Things are almost impossible for anyone to understand.

But to make some sort of effort, to give you an idea of what I'm going to be (or rather have been) talking about (because of course by the time you read this I will already be gone) I ask you a simple question:

ARE WE EVER REALLY HERE?

I mean, Chambers, man, have you ever noticed how we're

180

escaping all the time? ALL THE TIME!

Everywhere, I mean everywhere I look, I SEE NOTHING REAL! NOTHING AT ALL!

What are we about Chambers? What do our lives contain if we take away the distractions of alcohol, of weed, of television and computer games, of music?

Of the thoughts over which exam we're going to have to pass, of which career we're trying to carve out for ourselves or which job that's about to or has already begun to take over our lives,

Of which girl we're chasing at any particular moment in time, or of the girlfriend we're being so careful not to piss off, or get the hell away from so we can lose ourselves in some other bullshit, to find some mate and have some pointless conversation about a distraction we have in common?

WHAT THE HELL ARE WE CHAMBERS IF WE TAKE ALL THESE THINGS AWAY?

This is the question that's been screaming at me from all the corners of my world.

And when I ask myself what the hell we're avoiding, I think this is the answer. I think we're avoiding this thought. This question.

And this is the reason why I've been going up to the cliffs above the golf course lately.

I want to know if I'm really here you see. AND IF I AM I WANT TO EXPERIENCE THE FEELING OF THIS!

Nobody knows this Chambers but sometimes I stay up there well into the early hours of the morning. Listening to the fizzing, whooshing sounds of the wind and the sea. At one with the elements as you'll soon be putting it.

And it's peaceful up there as you can imagine.

But so far I can't say it's helped me come up with any solution to what's been fucking with my head completely.

And so what's going to happen up there tonight Chambers is something I never planned and that's completely out of my hands.

All we can really do Chambers is accept the fate of this.

181

You see when I walk up there tonight I have no intention of throwing myself off the top and ending my life.

It will happen and that is all.

AND IT'S NOT YOUR FAULT CHAMBERS! It's nobody's fault.

I'm already gone.

The weird thing is now that… well, memories are a funny thing. Like, even though I know I wrote this to myself I sometimes remember the letter as though Colin wrote it and gave it to me; slipped it into my pocket or something when I wasn't looking.

And I even have this weird recollection of finding it in my hoody later that evening, after I'd walked away from The Bowman, heading back on my way home, never to see Colin again.

FORTY-EIGHT

I dunno which of us left first. I know I'd been sitting there wanting to leave for quite a while but as to who got up initially I've no idea.

But yeah, next thing I knew, me and Colin were saying our, "See you later," stuff and walking off in our respective directions; him going through the town and over to the golf course I assume, while I was heading back home.

Everything was noticeably quiet on the walk back, apart from the wind; which had picked up a treat. But yeah it was weird for a Friday night with there not being a soul around – although thinking about the time, the fact the pubs weren't shut yet but were soon gonna be, I guess there was no purpose for anyone to be anywhere but in the pub or at home.

That is, apart from me and Colin of course. Colin making his way up to the cliffs while I was just walking back towards my house, and then for some reason I wasn't really feeling like going home all of a sudden, so I decided to see if Duncan was still up.

I turned left when I got to the corner shops at the bottom of my road and walked down Duncan's street, entertaining myself by picking out the few bedroom lights that were still lit, imagining and also half listening out for signs of any shagging action; although I didn't hear anything.

When I got to Duncan's flat there weren't any lights on, no sign of any life at all, which basically meant he was either out or had gone to bed. But I knocked anyway, rolling a fag while I sat on the doorstep, waiting for the response I knew wasn't gonna come.

And yeah, when I took out my lighter and sparked up I noticed a small bit of paper stuck on the door saying he'd, "Gone to London," and, "Back next week." And I remember laughing about that too 'cause of how, I dunno, just like it was sort of a reminder about how much everybody totally used his place as a social residence and all.

Anyway though, I thought about breaking in 'cause I still

183

didn't feel like going home but I didn't.

I headed down the beach instead. Dunno why. Possibly it's got something to do with Colin going up to the cliffs and maybe I wanted to do something similar – although saying that I'm not completely sure if this would've been the case 'cause I wasn't exactly feeling any like affiliation with Colin and his situation yet and had no idea of how he was soon gonna die.

But these days I do like to think I went down there for this reason 'cause, I dunno, like even though it's a bit weird to say, and totally can't be true, in the memory I have now I really was thinking about Colin at that moment and... well I have no idea of the exact time in which Colin jumped or fell off the cliff edge but I like to think of it being at the same moment as when I was sitting on the beach, staring out to sea, at the full moon and the stars, half-heartedly attempting to get to that point of, like allowing the simple reality of the world around me to, I dunno, fill my thoughts and stuff I guess; if you know what I mean.

*

Whether or not I actually took out the piece of paper and read it that night while I was sitting on the beach is of course something I know the answer to, 'cause I didn't.

I mean how could I have when it wasn't even written yet?

But strangely I do have this memory of taking Colin's (or rather my) note from the pocket of my Patterson hoody and reading it while I was there, sitting amongst the noise of the howling wind and smashing waves, calmly accepting what was happening or about to happen up on the cliffs I could see out in the distance before me.

But maybe this is a little overdramatic. More like a dream than something that actually would've happened.

Not that I didn't go down to the beach though, 'cause I did: I know this for definite.

And I sat there for about an hour I think; throwing stones in the sea, chilling out and not thinking about much at all for a hell of a long time actually.

Although eventually my imagination was going off on one, picturing all the people who'd soon be surrounding the place where I was sitting when the summer finally hit in: families out for a day in the sun, soaking up the heat, getting tanned, playing games, eating picnics and throwing balls around; generally just fucking about and having a good time.

Graz and his mates with their tins of beer, maybe the odd bit of music from the stereos a couple of groups had brought down, the sea full of people in swimming costumes, braving the cold water...

Typical English summer's day: everyone happy, carefree and all that shit.

FORTY-NINE

I was standing next to the cash machine with the hundred quid in my hand and the fizzing sound in my head again. The train station was opposite me.

I walked over there, towards the train station, tucking the money into my pocket and when I got through the double gate the train was in and I got on straight away. I'd only just sat down on the seat when the train started moving. And as soon as it pulled away the fizzing sound disappeared.

There was nobody in the carriage with me, I had it to myself. The window was to my left and I pressed my face against it, watching as the black reflection of the sea came into view between the trees that were slowly and then quickly moving past my face.

I still had the bottle of rum with me, still wrapped in the *Daily Argus* which I'd placed on the adjacent seat. I opened it up and took a swig. There wasn't much left any more and I figured I could finish it before I got to Firkinton (yeah it was like as this thought entered my head I realised I was actually gonna go there).

So I sat as the train moved on, drinking the rum, wondering what the night would bring and if I'd actually meet anyone; it was my first trip into Firkinton that summer.

I had the Lion Bar and then opened up the Fry's Chocolate Cream (both of which I'd bought at the offie earlier on) and took my time picking at this, staring at the window and thinking about stuff while outside the trees were soon turning into buildings – which I could see from the odd light coming from the rooms; mostly the window was just my reflection.

I reckon I'd been on the train a good twenty, thirty minutes before I finally opened up the job supplement and had a look.

The paper was pretty big and took me ages to unfold and properly organise. By the time I'd got it all folded up and easy to read I had ink all over my fingers. Yeah, everything in the *Argus* was black and white except the job section

186

which had reds and blues all over the place.

Despite the colour though there was nothing particularly interesting in the job pages; nothing at all. It was all, *Are You Looking for a Career in Sales?* And *Become a Driving Instructor* and a few positions with high salaries that I didn't understand and you probably needed experience for. I really wanted something to jump out at me (like, I totally *did*) but there really was nothing holding any of my interest for more than a couple of seconds and before I knew it I'd already finished the last page.

I mean, there was this big advert with a helicopter asking me to join the army which looked kinda cool. But no way in hell could I imagine myself getting up at five, six o'clock in the morning every day; or whatever time it is that they get up at. (And of course I'd seen enough war movies to realise it was probably a bad idea anyway).

There was this course in becoming a private investigator though, which I reckoned sounded quite interesting. Although, it was five-hundred quid and in Santersville, which is miles away from Bracksea and with no car and that, there wasn't much chance I could really imagine of it happening. And anyway, it was a *job* I needed.

So as I say, nothing really jumped out at me and before long I was back to daydreaming again about whatever the hell it was I was daydreaming about that night on my train ride in to Firkinton.

Actually, as I'm thinking about it now, the more I looked through the job section (to check there wasn't some great opportunity I'd missed), the more my eyes kept resting on the *Train to be a Private Investigator* advert actually, until finally I was simply draining the rum, staring at a picture of this giant magnifying glass, imagining myself in some cheap suit, maybe even a gun around my shoulder or in the glove compartment of some car I was sitting in, outside some block of flats with my camera on the seat next to me, waiting to catch some bird as she left or arrived with the husband of my client or whatever... (Not that telling the wife would do much good anyway).

When the conductor guy came into the carriage to ask for my ticket I was asleep. Lying there with the *Argus* on the floor next to me open on the job pages, the bottle of rum still clutched in one of my hands, three chocolate wrappers in front of me; and my head had sort of fallen over the edge of the seat: like, I can only imagine what he must've thought.

But he was okay and only asked for my ticket, which I didn't have so I said, "Can I buy one now?" and when he enquired as to where I'd got on I considered lying and saying, "Skipton," or something but instead simply told the truth and said, "Bracksea."

I took out my wad of money to give him ten pounds and he gave me the change, saying, "Off for a big night on the town then?" and I said, "Yeah."

Lightning Source UK Ltd.
Milton Keynes UK
UKOW050757300911

179551UK00001B/14/P

9 780953 317288